"You didn't hav[e]
Greer said after [...]
as your child."

"It was the right thing to do.[...]"

"Even though we didn't know for certain that Daisy is...was Layla's mother." She could think of half a dozen clients who wouldn't have done what he'd done.

"It was the right thing to do," he repeated after a moment.

Greer's chest squeezed. She reached across the table and covered both his hand and the bottle with hers. "I'm sorry, Ryder. I really am." That he lost his wife. That he'd become a father in such an unconventional way. That there were so many questions he surely had to have.

His jaw canted to one side. Then his blue eyes met hers and for some reason an oil slick of panic formed inside her. She started to pull her hand back, but he turned his palm upward and caught hers.

"Sorry enough to marry me?"

* * *

**RETURN TO THE DOUBLE C:
Under the big blue Wyoming sky,
this family discovers true love!**

Dear Reader,

"But what about baby Layla?"

Many readers have posed that question about the sweet baby who captured so many hearts in *Show Me a Hero* and *Yuletide Baby Bargain*.

I'm happy to say that Layla has a wonderful new home in *The Rancher's Christmas Promise*, very near the place where she'd once been mysteriously abandoned on a doorstep.

Responsibility is the only thing Ryder Wilson feels when the daughter of his onetime wife lands in his arms. Responsibility leads the single rancher to give the baby who may or may not be his child a home. Greer Templeton is more than willing to help him out when it becomes obvious he's overwhelmed, even to the point of marrying the guy. It's not romance. It's simply convenient. They've got their eyes wide open and focused on the only thing that matters—Layla.

Shows what two seemingly intelligent people know...

Come on along with Layla as Ryder remembers how to feel more than responsibility and Greer discovers that the best things in life are rarely convenient. And that this little family they're making is very real indeed.

I hope you will enjoy their enlightenment just as much as Layla and I did!

Allison

The Rancher's Christmas Promise

Allison Leigh

Recycling programs
for this product may
not exist in your area.

ISBN-13: 978-1-335-46605-1

The Rancher's Christmas Promise

Copyright © 2018 by Allison Lee Johnson

Printed in U.S.A.

www.Harlequin.com

Though her name is frequently on bestseller lists, **Allison Leigh**'s high point as a writer is hearing from readers that they laughed, cried or lost sleep while reading her books. She credits her family with great patience for the time she's parked at her computer, and for blessing her with the kind of love she wants her readers to share with the characters living in the pages of her books. Contact her at allisonleigh.com.

Books by Allison Leigh

Harlequin Special Edition

Return to the Double C

Show Me a Hero
Yuletide Baby Bargain
A Child Under His Tree
The BFF Bride
One Night in Weaver...
A Weaver Christmas Gift
A Weaver Beginning
A Weaver Vow

The Fortunes of Texas: The Rulebreakers

Fortune's Homecoming

The Fortunes of Texas: The Secret Fortunes

Wild West Fortune

The Fortunes of Texas: All Fortune's Children

Fortune's Secret Heir

Visit the Author Profile page
at Harlequin.com for more titles.

For my family.

Prologue

"You've got to be kidding me."

Ryder Wilson stared at the people on his porch. Even before they introduced themselves, he'd known the short, skinny woman was a cop thanks to the Braden Police Department badge she was wearing. But the two men with her? He'd never seen them before.

And after the load of crap they'd just spewed, he'd like to never see them again.

"We're not kidding, Mr. Wilson." That came from the serious-looking bald guy. The one who looked like he was a walking heart attack, considering the way he kept mopping the sweat off his face even though it was freezing outside. March had roared in like a lion this year, bringing with it a major snowstorm. Ryder hadn't lived there that long—it was only his second winter there—but people around town said they hadn't seen anything like it in Braden for more than a decade.

All he knew was that the snow was piled three feet high, making his life these days even more challenging. Making him wonder why he'd ever chosen Wyoming over New Mexico in the first place. Yeah, they got snow in Taos. But not like this.

"We believe that the infant girl who's been under our protection since she was abandoned three months ago is your daughter." The man tried to look past Ryder's shoulder. "Perhaps we could discuss this inside?"

Ryder had no desire to invite them in. But one of them *was* a cop. He hadn't crossed purposes with the law before and he wasn't real anxious to do so now. Didn't mean he had to like it, though.

His aunt hadn't raised him to be slob. She'd be horrified if she ever knew strangers were seeing the house in its current state.

He slapped his leather gloves together. He had chores waiting for him. But he supposed a few minutes wouldn't make much difference. "Don't think there's much to discuss," he warned as he stepped out of the doorway. He folded his arms across his chest, standing pretty much in their way so they had to crowd together in the small space where he dumped his boots. Back home, his aunt Adelaide would call the space a *vestibule*. Here, it wasn't so formal; he'd carved out his home from a converted barn. "I appreciate your concern for an abandoned baby, but whoever's making claims I fathered a child is out of their mind." Once burned, twice shy. Another thing his aunt was fond of saying.

The cop's brown eyes looked pained. "Ryder—may I call you Ryder?" She didn't wait for his permission, but plowed right on, anyway. "I'm sorry we have to be the bearer of bad news, but we believe your wife was the baby's mother, and—"

At the word *wife*, what had been Ryder's already-thin patience went by the wayside. "My *wife* ran out on me a year ago. Whatever she's done since is her prob—"

"Not anymore," the dark-haired guy said.

"What'd you say your name was?" Ryder met the other man's gaze head-on, knowing perfectly well he hadn't said his name. The pretty cop's role there was obviously official. Same with the sweaty bald guy—he had to be from social services. But the third intruder? The guy who was watching him as though he'd already formed an opinion—a bad one?

"Grant Cooper." The man's voice was flat. "Karen's my sister."

"There's your problem," Ryder responded just as flatly. "My so-called *wife's* name was Daisy. Daisy Miranda. You've got the wrong guy." He pointedly reached around them for the door to show them out. "So if you'll excuse me, I've got ice to break so my animals can get at their water."

"This is Karen." Only because she was a little slip of a thing, the cop succeeded in maneuvering between him and the door. She held a wallet-sized photo up in front of his face.

Ryder's nerves tightened even more than when he'd first opened the door to find these people on his front porch.

He didn't want to touch the photograph or examine it. He didn't need to. He recognized his own face just fine. In the picture, he'd been kissing the wedding ring he'd just put on Daisy's finger. The wedding had been a whirlwind sort of thing, like everything else about their relationship. Three months start to finish, from the moment they met outside the bar where she'd just quit her job until the day she'd walked out on him two weeks after their wedding. That's how long it had taken to meet, get hitched and get unhitched.

Though the unhitching part was still a work in progress. Not that he'd been holding on to hope that she'd return. But he'd had other things more important keeping him occupied than getting a formal divorce. Namely the Diamond-L ranch, which he'd purchased only a few months before meeting her. His only regret was that he hadn't kept his attention entirely on the ranch all along. It would have saved him some grief. "Where'd you get that?"

The cop asked her own question. "Can you confirm this is you and your wife in this picture?"

His jaw felt tight. "Yeah." Unfortunately. The Las Vegas wedding chapel had given them a cheap set of pictures. Ryder had tossed all of them in the fireplace, save the one the cop was holding now. He'd mailed that one to Daisy in response to a stupid postcard he'd gotten from her six months after she'd left him. A postcard on which she'd written only the words *I'm sorry.*

He still wasn't sure what she'd meant. Sorry for leaving him without a word or warning? Or sorry she'd ever married him in the first place?

"You wrote this?" The cop had turned the photo over, revealing his handwriting on the back. *So much for vows.*

Ryder was actually a little surprised that it was so legible, considering how drunk he'd been at the time he'd sent the photo. He nodded once.

The cop looked sympathetic. "I'm sorry to say that she died in a car accident over New Year's."

He waited as the words sank in. Expecting to feel something. Was he supposed to feel bad? Maybe he did. He wasn't sure. He'd known Daisy was a handful from the get-go. So when she took a powder the way she had, it shouldn't have been as much of a shock as it had been.

But one thing was certain. Everything that Daisy had told him had been a lie. From start to finish.

He might be an uncomplicated guy, but he understood the bottom line facing him now. "And you want to pawn off her baby on me." He looked the dark-haired guy in the face again. "Or do you just want money?" He lifted his arm, gesturing with the worn leather gloves. "Look around. All I've got is what you see. And it'll be a cold day in hell before I let a couple strangers making claims like yours get one finger on it."

Grant's eyes looked like flint. "As usual, my sister's taste in men was worse than—"

"Gentlemen." The other man mopped his forehead again, giving both Ryder and Grant wary looks even as he took a step between them. "Let's keep our cool. The baby is our focus."

Ryder ignored him. He pointed at Grant. "My wife never even told me she had a brother."

"My sister never told me she had a husband."

"The situation is complicated enough," the cop interrupted, "without the two of you taking potshots at each other." Her expression was troubled, but her voice was calm. And Ryder couldn't miss the way she'd wrapped her hand familiarly around Grant's arm. "Ray is right. What's important here is the baby."

"Yes. The baby under our protection." Ray was obviously hoping to maintain control over the discussion. "There is no local record of the baby's birth. Our only way left to establish who the child's parents are is through you, Mr. Wilson. We've expended every other option."

"You don't even *know* the baby was hers?"

Ray looked pained. Grant looked like he wanted to punch something. Hell, maybe even Ryder. The cop just looked worried.

"The assumption is that your wife was the person to have left the baby at the home her former employer, Jaxon Swift, shared with his brother, Lincoln," she said.

"Now, that *does* sound like Daisy." Ryder knew he sounded bitter. "I only knew her a few months, but it was still long enough to learn she's good at running out on people."

Maybe he did feel a little bad about Daisy. He hadn't gotten around to divorcing his absent wife. Now, if what these people said were true, he wouldn't need to. Instead of being a man with a runaway wife, he was a man with a deceased one. There was probably something wrong with him for not feeling like his world had just been rocked. "But maybe you're wrong. She wasn't pregnant when she left me," he said bluntly. He couldn't let himself believe otherwise.

"Would you agree to a paternity test?"

"The court can compel you, Mr. Wilson," Ray added when Ryder didn't answer right away.

It was the wrong tack for Ray to take. Ryder had been down the whole paternity-accusation path before. He hadn't taken kindly to it then, and he wasn't inclined to now. "Daisy was my wife, loose as that term is in this case. A baby born to her during our marriage makes me the presumed father, whether there's a test or not. But you don't know that the baby was actually hers. You just admitted it. Which tells me the court probably isn't on your side as much as you're implying. Unless I say otherwise, and without you knowing who this baby's mother is, I'm just a guy in a picture."

"We should have brought Greer," Grant said impatiently to the cop. "She's used to guys like him."

But the cop wasn't listening to Grant. She was looking at Ryder with an earnest expression. "You aren't just a guy in a picture. You're our best hope for preventing the child we believe is Grant's niece from being adopted by strangers."

That's when Ryder saw that she'd reached out to clasp Grant's hand, their fingers entwined. So, she had a dog in this race.

He thought about pointing out that he was a stranger to them, too, no matter what sort of guy Grant had deemed Ryder to be. "And if I cooperated and the test confirms I'm *not* this baby's father, you still wouldn't have proof that Daisy is—" *dammit* "—was the baby's mother."

"If the test is positive, then we know she was," Ray said. "Without your cooperation, the proof of Karen's maternity is circumstantial. We admit that. But you were her husband. There's no putative father. If you even suspected she'd become pregnant during your marriage, your very existence is enough to establish legal paternity, DNA proof or not."

The cop looked even more earnest. "And the court can't proceed with an adoption set in motion by Layla's abandonment."

The name startled him. *"Layla!"*

The three stared at him with varying degrees of surprise and expectation.

"Layla was my mother's name." His voice sounded gruff, even to his own ears. Whatever it was that Daisy had done with her child, using that name was a sure way of making sure he'd get involved. After only a few months together, she'd learned enough about him to know that.

He exhaled roughly. Slapped his leather gloves together. Then he stepped out of the way so he wasn't blocking them from the rest of his home. "You'd better come inside and sit." He felt weary all of a sudden. As if everything he'd accomplished in his thirty-four years was for nothing. What was that song? "There Goes My Life."

"I expect this is gonna take a while to work out." He glanced at the disheveled room, with its leather couch and oversize, wall-mounted television. That's what happened when a man spent more time tending cows than he did anything else. He'd even tended some of them in this very room.

Fortunately, his aunt Adelaide would never need to know.

"You'll have to excuse the mess, though."

Chapter One

Five months later.

The August heat was unbearable.

The forecasters kept saying the end of the heat wave was near, but Greer Templeton had lost faith in them. She twisted in her seat, trying to find the right position that allowed her to feel the cold air from the car vents on more than two square inches of her body. It wasn't as if she could pull up her skirt so the air could blow straight up her thighs or pull down her blouse so the air could get at the rest of her.

She'd tried that once, only to find herself the object of interest of a leering truck driver with a clear view down into her car. If she'd never seen or heard from the truck driver again, it wouldn't have been so bad. Instead, she'd had the displeasure of serving as the driver's public defender not two days later when he was charged with littering.

"I hate August!" she yelled, utterly frustrated.

Nobody heard.

The other vehicles crawling along the narrow, curving stretch of highway between Weaver—where she'd just come from a frustrating visit with a new client in jail—and Braden all had their windows closed against the oppressive heat, the same way she did.

It was thirty miles, give or take, between Braden and Weaver, and she drove it several times every week. Sometimes more than once in a single day. She knew the highway like the back of her hand. Where the infrequent passing zones were, where the dips filled with ice in the winter and where the shoulder was treacherous. She knew that mile marker 12 had the best view into Braden and mile marker 3 was the spot you were most likely to get a speeding ticket.

The worst, though, was grinding up and down the hills, going around the curves at a crawl because she was stuck behind a too-wide truck hogging the roadway with a too-tall load of hay.

Impatience raged inside her and she pushed her fingers against one of the car vents, feeling the air blast against her palm. It didn't provide much relief, because it was barely cool.

Probably because her car was close to overheating, she realized.

Even as she turned off the AC and rolled down the windows, a cloud billowed from beneath the front hood of her car.

She wanted to scream.

Instead, she coasted onto the weedy shoulder. It was barely wide enough.

The car behind her laid on its horn as it swerved around her.

"I hate August!" she yelled after it while her vehicle burped out steam into the already-miserable air.

So much for getting to Maddie's surprise baby shower early.

Ali was never going to forgive Greer. Unlike their sister, Maddie, the soul of patience she was not. Just that morning Ali had called to remind Greer of her tasks where the shower was concerned. It had been the fifth such call in as many days.

Marrying Grant hadn't softened Ali's annoying side at all.

Greer wasn't going to chance exiting through the driver's side because of the traffic, so she hitched up her skirt enough to climb over the console and out the passenger-side door.

In just the few minutes it took to get out of the car and open up the hood, Greer's silk blouse was glued to her skin by the perspiration sliding down her spine.

The engine had stopped spewing steam. But despite her father's best efforts to teach the triplets the fundamentals of car care when she and her sisters were growing up, what lived beneath the hood of Greer's car was still a mystery.

She knew from experience there was no point in checking her cell phone for a signal. There were about four points on the thirty-mile stretch where a signal reliably reached, and this spot wasn't one of them. If a Good Samaritan didn't happen to stop, she knew the schedules of both the Braden Police Department and the Weaver Sheriff's Department. Even if her disabled vehicle wasn't reported by someone passing by, officers from one or the other agency routinely traveled the roadway even on a hot August Saturday. She didn't expect it would be too long before she had some help.

She popped the trunk a few inches so the heat wouldn't build up any more than it already had and left the windows down. Then she walked along the shoulder until she reached an outcrop of rock that afforded a little shade from the sun and toed off her shoes, not even caring that she was probably ruining her silk blouse by leaning against the jagged stone.

Sorry, Ali.

Ryder saw the slender figure in white before he saw the car. It almost made him do a double take, the way sailors did when they spotted a mermaid sunning herself on a rock. A second look reassured him that lack of sleep hadn't caused him to start hallucinating.

Not yet, anyway.

She was on the opposite side of the road, and there was no place for him to pull his rig around to get to her. So he kept on driving until he reached his original destination—the turnoff to the Diamond-L. As soon as he did, he turned around and pulled back out onto the highway to head back to her.

It was only a matter of fifteen minutes.

The disabled foreign car was still sitting there, like a strange out-of-place insect among the pickup trucks rumbling by every few minutes. He parked behind it, but let his engine idle and kept the air-conditioning on. He propped his arm over the steering column and thumbed back his hat as he studied the woman.

She'd noticed him and was picking her way through the rough weeds back toward her car.

He'd recognized her easily enough.

Greer Templeton. One of the identical triplets who'd turned his life upside down. Starting with the cop, Ali, who'd come to his door five months ago.

It wasn't entirely their fault.

They weren't responsible for abandoning Layla. That was his late wife.

Now Layla was going through nannies like there was a revolving door on the nursery. Currently, the role was filled by Tina Lewis. She'd lasted two weeks but was already making dissatisfied noises.

He blew out a breath and checked the road before pushing open his door and getting out of the truck. "Looks like you've got a problem."

"Ryder?"

He spread his hands. "'Fraid so." Any minute she'd ask about the baby and he wasn't real sure what he would say.

For nearly five months—ever since Judge Stokes had officially made Layla his responsibility—the Templeton triplets had tiptoed around him. He'd quickly learned how attached they'd become to the baby, caring for her after Daisy dumped her on a "friend's" porch.

Supposedly, his wife hadn't been sleeping with that friend but Ryder still had his doubts. DNA might have ruled out Jaxon Swift as Layla's father, but the man owned Magic Jax, the bar where Daisy had briefly worked as a cocktail waitress before they'd met. He would never understand why she hadn't just come to *him* if she'd needed help. He had been her husband, for God's sake. Not her onetime boss. Unless she'd been more involved with Jax than they all had admitted.

As for the identity of Layla's real father, everyone had been happy as hell to stop wondering as soon as Ryder gave proof that he and Daisy had been married.

Didn't mean Ryder hadn't wondered, though.

But doing a DNA test at this point wouldn't change

anything where he was concerned. It would prove Layla was his by blood. Or it wouldn't.

Either way, he believed she was his wife's child.

Which made Layla his responsibility. Period.

The questions about Daisy, though? Every time he looked at Layla, they bubbled up inside him.

For now, though, he focused on Greer.

It was no particular hardship.

The Templeton triplets scored pretty high in the looks department. He could tell Greer apart from her twins because she always looked a little more sophisticated. Maddie—the social worker who'd been Layla's foster mother—had long hair reaching halfway down her back. Ali—the cop who'd shown up on his doorstep—had blond streaks. And he'd never seen her dressed in anything besides her police uniform.

Greer, though?

Her dark hair barely reached her shoulders and not a single strand was ever out of place. She was a lawyer and dressed the part in skinny skirts with expensive-looking jackets and high heels that looked more big-city than Wyoming dirt. She'd been the one who'd ushered him through all the legalities with the baby. And she was the only one of her sisters who hadn't been openly crying when they'd brought Layla and all of her stuff out to his ranch to turn her over to his care. But there'd been no denying the emotion in her eyes. She just hadn't allowed herself the relief of tears.

For some reason, that had seemed worse.

Ryder had been uncomfortable as hell with so much female emotion. Greer's most of all.

He'd rather have to deal with the general animosity Daisy's brother clearly felt for him. That, at least, was straightforward and simple. Grant's sister was dead. Whether he'd voiced it outright or not, he blamed Ryder.

Since Ryder was already shouldering the blame, it didn't make any difference to him.

Now Greer was shading her eyes with one hand and holding her hair off her neck with the other. Instead of asking about Layla first thing, though, she stopped near the front bumper of her car. "It overheated. I saw steam coming out from the hood and pulled off as soon as I could."

He joined her in front of the car. He knew the basics when it came to engines—enough to keep the machinery on his ranch running without too much outside help—but he was a lot more comfortable with the anatomy of horses and cows. "How long have you been sitting out here?"

"Too long." She plucked the front of her blouse away from her throat and glanced at the watch circling her narrow wrist. "I thought someone would stop sooner than this. Ali'll think I'm deliberately late."

The only heat from the engine came from the sun glaring down on it. He checked a few of the hoses and looked underneath for signs of leaking coolant, but the ground beneath the car was dry. "Why's that?"

"We're throwing a surprise baby shower for Maddie today. I'm supposed to help set up."

"Didn't know she was pregnant." He straightened. It was impossible to miss the sharpness in Greer's brown eyes.

"Why would you, when you've been avoiding all of us since March?"

"Some law that says I needed to do otherwise?" He hadn't been avoiding them entirely. Just…mostly.

It had been easy, considering he had a ranch to run.

She pursed her bow-shaped lips. "You know my family has a vested interest in Layla. At the very least, you could try accepting an invitation or two when they're extended."

"Maybe I'm too busy to accept invitations." He waited a beat. "I am a single father, you know."

If he wasn't mistaken, her eye actually twitched.

She'd always struck him as the one most tightly wound.

It was too bad that he also couldn't look at her without wondering just what it would take to *un*wind her.

He closed the hood of her car with a firm hand. "You want to try starting her up? See what happens with the temperature gauge?"

He thought she might argue—if only for the sake of it—but she opened the passenger door. Then he had to choke back a laugh when she climbed across and into the driver's seat, where she started the engine. Her focus was clearly on her dashboard and he could tell the gauge was rising just by the frown on her face.

She shut off the engine again and looked through the windshield. "Needle went straight to the red." She climbed back out the passenger side.

"Something wrong with the driver's-side door?"

She was looking down at herself as she got out, tweaking that white skirt hugging her slender hips until it hung smooth and straight. "No, but I don't want it getting hit by a passing vehicle if I open it."

He eyed the distance between the edge of the road and where she'd pulled off on the shoulder. "Real cautious of you."

"I'm a lawyer. I'm always cautious."

"Overly so, I'd say." Not that he hadn't enjoyed the show. She was a little skinny for his taste, but he couldn't deny she was a looker. He pulled off his cowboy hat long enough to swipe his arm across his fore-head. "I can drive you into town, or I can send a tow out for you." He didn't have time to do both, because he had to be back at the ranch before the nanny left or his housekeeper, Mrs. Pyle, would have kittens. "What's your choice?"

Greer swallowed her frustration. Considering Ryder Wilson's standoffishness since they'd met, she was a little surprised that he'd stopped to assist at all.

As soon as she'd realized who was driving the enor-mous pickup truck pulling up behind her car, she'd been torn between anticipation and the desire to cry *what next?*

It was entirely annoying that the brawny, blue-eyed rancher was the first man to make her hormones sit up and take notice in too long a while.

Annoying and impossible to act on, considering the strange nature of their acquaintance.

All she wanted to do was ask Ryder how Layla was doing. But Maddie had been insistent that none of them intrude on him too soon.

They'd all been wrapped around Layla's tiny little finger and none more than Maddie, who'd been caring for her nearly the whole while before Ali discovered Ry-der's existence. Yet it was Maddie who'd urged them to give Ryder time. To adjust. To adapt. They knew Ryder was taking decent care of the baby he'd claimed, be-cause Maddie's boss, Raymond Marx, checked up on him for a while at first, so he could report back to the courts. Give Ryder time, Maddie insisted, and eventu-ally he would see the benefit of letting them past his walls.

Didn't mean that it had been easy.

Didn't mean it was easy now, not dashing over to the truck to see Layla.

She didn't know if it was that prospect that made her feel so shaky inside, or if it was because of Layla's brown-haired daddy. She wasn't sure she even liked Ryder all that much.

Yes, he'd been legally named Layla's father and yes, he'd taken responsibility for her. But there was an edge to him that had rubbed Greer wrong from the very first time they met. She just hadn't been able to pinpoint why.

"If you don't mind driving me into town," she managed, "I'd be grateful."

The brim of his hat dipped briefly. "Probably should lock her up." He started for his big truck parked behind the car.

She watched him walk away. He was wearing blue jeans and a checked shirt with the sleeves rolled up to his elbows. Except for when he'd briefly swiped an arm over his forehead, he appeared unaffected by the sweltering day.

"Probably should lock her up," she parroted childishly under her breath. As if she didn't have the sense to know that without being told.

She retrieved her purse and briefcase from the back seat, looping the long straps over her shoulder, then warily lifted the trunk lid higher. The shower cake that she'd nestled carefully between two boxes full of work from the office amazingly didn't look too much the worse for wear. It was a delightful amalgam of block and ball shapes, frosted in white, yellow and blue. How Tabby Clay had balanced them all together like that was a mystery to Greer.

She was just glad to see that the creation hadn't

melted into a puddle of goo while she'd waited on the side of the road.

She carefully lifted the white board with the heavy cake on top out of the trunk and gingerly carried it toward Ryder's truck. Her heart was beating so hard, she could hear it inside her head. The last time she'd seen Layla had been at Shop-World in Weaver, when she'd taken a client shopping for an affordable set of clothes to wear for trial, and Ryder had been in the next checkout line over, buying diapers, coffee and whiskey.

Layla had been asleep in the cart. Greer had noticed that her blond curls had gotten a reddish cast, but the stuffed pony she'd clutched was the same one Greer had given her for Valentine's Day.

It had been all she could do not to pluck the baby out of the cart and cuddle her close. Instead, after a stilted exchange with Ryder, she'd hustled her client through the checkout so fast that he'd wondered out loud if she'd slid through without paying for something. *No. That's what* you *like to do*, she'd told him as she'd rushed him out the door.

But now, when she got close enough to Ryder's truck to see inside, her feet dragged to a halt.

There was no car seat.

Definitely no Layla.

The disappointment that swamped her was so searing, it put the hot afternoon sun to shame. Her eyes stung and she blinked hard, quickening her pace once more only to feel her heel slide on the loose gravel. The heavy cake started tipping one way and she leveled the board, even as her shoulder banged against the side of his truck.

She froze, holding her breath as she held the cake board aloft.

"What the hell are you doing over here?"

She was hot. Sweaty. And brokenhearted that she wasn't getting a chance to see sweet Layla.

"What do you care?" she snapped back. She was still holding the cake straight out from her body, and the weight of it was considerable. "Just open the door, would you please? If I don't deliver this thing in one piece, Ali's going to skin me alive."

He gave her a wide berth as he reached around her to open the door of the truck. "Let me take it." His hands covered hers where she held the board, and she jerked as if he'd prodded her with a live wire.

Her face went hot. "I don't need your help."

He let go and held his hands up in the air. "Whatever." He backed away.

Nobody liked to feel self-conscious. Not even her.

She turned away from him to set the cake board inside the truck, but it was too big to fit on the floor, which meant she'd have to hold it on her lap.

Greer heaved out a breath and looked at Ryder. He wordlessly took the cake long enough for her to dump her briefcase and purse on the floor, and climb up on the high seat.

"All settled now?" His voice was mild.

For some reason, it annoyed her more than if he'd made some snarky comment.

Unfortunately, that's when she realized that she'd left her trunk open and the car unlocked.

She slid off the seat again, mentally cursing ranchers and their too-big trucks as she jumped out onto the ground. Ignoring the amused glint in his dark blue eyes, she strode past him, grinding her teeth when her heel again slid on the loose gravel.

She'd have landed on her butt if not for the quick hand he shot out to steady her.

She shrugged off his touch as if she'd been burned but managed a grudging "thank you." It figured that he could manage to hold on to the heavy cake and still keep her from landing on her butt.

She finally made it to her car without further mishap and secured it. The passenger door of his truck was still open and waiting for her when she returned.

She climbed inside and fastened the safety belt. Then he settled the enormous, heavy cake on her lap, taking an inordinate amount of time before sliding his big, warm hands away.

As soon as he did, she yanked the door closed.

The cool air flowed from the air-conditioning vents.

It was the only bright spot, and gave a suitable reason for the shivers that skipped down her spine.

She wrapped her hands firmly around the edge of the cake board to hold it in place while Ryder circled the front of the truck and got in behind the wheel.

His blue eyes skated over and she shivered again. Despite the heat. Despite the perspiration soaking her blouse.

Annoyance swelled inside her.

"I hope you have someone decent watching Layla."

His expression turned chilly. "I've got plenty of things I needed to be doing besides stopping to help you out. You really want to go there?"

She pressed her lips together. If Maddie ever found out she'd been rude to Ryder, her sister would never forgive her.

"Just drive," she said ungraciously.

He lifted an eyebrow slightly.

God. She really hated feeling self-conscious.

"Please," she added.

He waited a beat. "Better." Then he put the truck in gear.

Chapter Two

"I knew you'd be late."

Greer ignored Ali's greeting as she entered the stately old mansion that Maddie shared with her husband, Lincoln Swift. She kicked the heavy front door closed, blocking out the sound of Ryder's departing truck. Passing the round table in the foyer loaded down with fancifully wrapped gifts and the grand wooden staircase, she headed into the dining room with the cake.

The sight of a cheerfully decorated sheet cake already sitting in the middle of the table shredded her last nerve.

She stared over her shoulder at Ali. Her sister looked uncommonly pretty in a bright yellow sundress. More damningly, Ali was as cool and fresh as the daisy she'd stuck in her messy ponytail. "You have a *backup* cake?"

"Of course I have a backup cake." Ali waved her hands, and the big diamond rock that Grant had put on her ring finger a few months earlier glinted in the sunlight shining through the mullioned windows. "Because I knew you would be late! You're always late, because you're always working for that slave driver over at the dark side."

"Well, I wouldn't have *been* late, if I hadn't broken down on the way back from Weaver! Now would you move that stupid cake so I can put this one down where it belongs?"

"Girls!" Their mother, Meredith, dashed into the dining room, accompanied by the usual tinkle of tiny bells on the ankle bracelet she wore. "This is supposed to be a party." She tsked. "You're thirty years old and you still sound as if you're bickering ten-year-olds." She whisked the offending backup cake off the table. "Ali, put this in the kitchen."

Ali took the sheet cake from their mother and crossed her eyes at Greer behind their mother's back while Greer set Tabby's masterpiece in its place.

"It's just beautiful," Meredith exclaimed, clasping her hands together. Despite her chastisement, her eyes were sparkling. "Maddie's going to love it." As she turned away, the dark hair she'd passed on to her daughters danced in corkscrew curls nearly to the small of her back. "It's just too bad that Tabby wasn't able to come to the party."

"If Gracie weren't running a fever, she'd have brought the cake herself." Greer glanced around. "Obviously Ali didn't have a problem decorating without me. It looks like the baby-shower fairy threw up in here." The raindrop theme was in full force. Silver and white balloons hovered above the table in a cluster of "clouds" from which shimmering crystal raindrops hung down,

drifting slightly in the cool room. It was sweet and sub-
tly chic and just like Maddie. Altogether perfect, really.

As usual, Ali hadn't really needed Greer at all.

Meredith squeezed her arm as if she'd read her mind.
"Stop sweating the details, Greer. You had a hand in the
planning of this, whether you were here to help pull it
together this afternoon or not. Now—" she eyed Greer
more closely "—what's this about your car breaking
down?"

It was a timely reminder that she probably looked as
bedraggled as she felt. A glance at her watch told her
the guests would be arriving in a matter of minutes.
Linc was supposed to be delivering Maddie—hopefully
still in the dark about the surprise—shortly after that.

"The car overheated. I left it locked up on the side
of the road."

"How'd you get here?"

She felt reluctant to say, knowing the mention of
Ryder would only remind them all of how much they
missed Layla. "Someone stopped and gave me a ride to
town. I'll arrange a tow after the shower." She dashed
her hand down the front of her outfit and headed for
the stairs. "I need to put on something less wrinkled
and sweaty. Hopefully there's more than just maternity
clothes in Maddie's closet." She hadn't made it halfway
up the staircase before the doorbell rang and she could
hear Ali greeting the new arrivals.

She darted up the rest of the stairs.

Even after more than half a year, it was hard to get
used to the fact that Maddie lived in this grand old
house with Linc. The place had belonged to his and
Jax's grandmother Ernestine. When the triplets were
children, Meredith had cleaned house for Ernestine.

Greer and her sisters had often accompanied her. Now, Jax no longer shared the house with Linc. Maddie did.

She entered the big walk-in closet, mentally sending an apology to her brother-in-law for the intrusion. She knew that Maddie wouldn't mind. Not surprisingly, most of the clothes hanging on the rods were designed for a woman who looked about a hundred months pregnant.

She could hear the doorbell chime again downstairs and quickly flipped through the hangers, finally pulling out a colorful dress she remembered Maddie wearing for Easter, when she'd had just a small baby bump. The dress had a stretchy waist that was a little loose on Greer, but it would do.

She changed and flipped her hair up into a clip. If there'd been blond streaks in her hair, she'd look just like Ali. Tousled and carefree.

But Greer hadn't felt carefree in what was starting to feel like forever.

She stared at her reflection and plucked at the loose waist of the dress. Maddie was pregnant. Now Ali and Grant were married. Considering how the two couldn't keep their hands off each other, it was only a matter of time before they were starting a family, too.

But Greer?

The last date she'd had that had gotten even remotely physical was more than two years ago, so if she wanted a baby, she was going to need either a serious miracle or big-time artificial intervention. As it was, the little birth control implant she had in her arm was pretty much pointless.

From downstairs, she heard a peal of laughter. Turning away from her reflection, she headed down to join them. She might not feel carefree, but she *was* thrilled about Maddie's coming baby. So she would put on a party face for that reason alone.

And she would try to forget that Ali had gotten a damn backup cake.

Ryder stared at Doreen Pyle. "What do you mean, you're quitting?"

"Just that, Ryder." Mrs. Pyle continued scooping mushy green food into Layla's mouth, even though the little girl kept twisting her head away. "When you hired me, it was to be your housekeeper. Not your nanny."

"That's because I *had* a nanny." His voice was tight. "Look, I'm sorry that Tina took a hike this afternoon with no warning." At least the others who'd come before her had given him some notice. "I'll start looking again first thing tomorrow."

"It won't matter, Ryder. Nobody wants to live all the way out here." She finally gave up on the green mush and glanced at him. The look in her lined eyes was more sympathetic than her tone had been. "You need to give up the idea of a live-in nanny, Ryder. Or else give up the idea of a housekeeper. You can't afford both."

He could, if he were willing to dip into his savings. But he wasn't willing. Any more than he was willing to take Adelaide's money. She'd made her way on her own, and he was doing the same. On his own. But if he were going to continue growing this small ranch, he couldn't be carting a growing baby around everywhere while he worked. "I'll give you another raise." He'd already given her one. "Stay on and take care of Layla. You're good with her. I'll hire someone to help with the housekeeping."

"I don't want to live out here, either." She pushed off her chair, wincing a little as she straightened. "The only difference between me and Tina is that I won't take off while your back is turned." She grabbed a cloth and started wiping up Layla's face. The baby squirmed, trying to avoid the cloth just like she'd tried to avoid the green muck. But Mrs. Pyle prevailed and then tossed the cloth aside. "You don't need a nanny around the clock, anyway. You're here at night." She lifted the baby out of the high chair. "You can take care of her yourself. Then just get some help during the day. Preferably someone who doesn't have to drive farther than from Braden, or once the winter comes, you're going to have problems all over again." She plopped Layla into his arms and hustled to the sink where she wet another cloth. "But it won't be me. I have my own family I need to look out for, too. My grandson—" She broke off, grimacing. She squeezed out the moisture and waved the rag at him. "I won't apologize for not wanting to be tied down to a baby all over again. Not at my age." She sounded defensive.

"I don't need an apology, Mrs. Pyle. I need someone to take care of Layla!"

The baby lightly slapped his face with her hands and laughed.

Mrs. Pyle's expression softened. She chucked Layla lightly under the chin. "Maybe instead of looking for a nanny, you should start looking for a mama for this little girl."

Ryder grimaced.

"There are plenty of other fish in the sea. All you need to do is cast your line. You're a good-looking cuss when you clean yourself up. Someone'll come biting before you know it."

"I don't think so." One foray into so-called wedded bliss was one disaster enough.

The look in Doreen's eyes got even more sympathetic. "I know what it's like to lose a spouse, hon. Single parents might be all the rage these days, but I'm here to tell you it's easier when two people are committed to their family. You're still young. You don't want to spend the rest of your life alone. I'm sure your poor wife wouldn't have wanted that, either. She'd surely want this little mite to have a proper mama. Someone who won't toss aside caring for Layla on some flighty whim the way Tina just did."

He managed a tight smile. His "poor wife" had been exactly that. A poor wife. But not in the way Doreen Pyle meant. Abandoning Layla had been a helluva way to show off her maternal nature. Tina's quitting out of the blue was a lot more forgivable. "Would you at least stay until I find someone new?" He had to finish getting the hay in before the weather turned. And then he and his closest neighbor to the east were helping each other through roundup. Then he'd be sorting and shipping and—

"I'll stay another week," she said, interrupting the litany of tasks running through his mind. "But that's it, Ryder."

Layla grinned up at him with her six teeth and smacked his face again with her hand.

He looked back at his housekeeper. "A week."

"That's all the time I can give you, Ryder. I'm sorry."

A week was better than nothing.

And it was damn sure more than Tina had given him.

"I don't suppose you could stay and watch Layla for another few hours or so?" As his housekeeper began shaking her head no, he grabbed the refrigerator door and stuck his head inside, so he could pretend he didn't see. "Got a friend—" big overstatement there "—who needs help towing her car back to town. Broke down up near Devil's Crossing." He grabbed the bottle of ketchup that Layla latched onto and stuck it back on the refrigerator shelf. She immediately reached for something else and he quickly shut the door and gave Mrs. Pyle a hopeful look. The same one he'd mastered by the time he was ten and living with Adelaide.

Instead of looking resigned and accepting, though, Mrs. Pyle was giving him an eyebrows-in-the-hairline look. "*Her* car? Is this female friend single?"

Warning alarms went off inside his head. "Yeah."

She lifted Layla out of his arms. "Well, go rescue your lady friend. And give my suggestion about a wife some thought."

He let her remark slide. "Thank you, Mrs. Pyle."

"Not going to change my leaving in a week," she warned as she carried the baby out of the kitchen. "And you might think about washing some of the day off yourself, as well, before you go out playing Dudley Do-Right."

He hadn't showered, but he *had* washed up and pulled on fresh clothes. And he still felt pretty stupid about it.

It wasn't as if he wanted to impress Greer Templeton. Not with a clean shirt or anything else. And it damn sure wasn't as if he was giving Mrs. Pyle's suggestion any consideration.

Marrying someone just for Layla's sake?

He pushed the idea straight out of his mind and shifted into Park at the top of the hill as he stared out at the worn-looking Victorian house.

The white paint on the fancy trim was peeling and the dove-gray paint on the siding was fading. The shingle roof needed repair, if not replacement, and the brick chimney looked as if it were related to the Leaning Tower of Pisa. But the yard around the house was green and neat.

Not exactly what he would have expected of the lady lawyer. But then again, she worked for the public defender's office, where the pay was reportedly abysmal and most of her clients were supposedly the dregs of society.

He turned off the engine and got out of the truck, walking around to the trailer he'd used to haul Greer's little car. He checked the chains holding it in place and then headed up the front walk to the door.

The street was quiet, and his boots clumped loudly as he went up the steps and crossed the porch to knock on the door. The heavy brass door knocker was shaped like a dragonfly.

If he could ever get Adelaide to come and visit Braden, she'd love the place.

When no one came to the door, he went back down the porch steps. There was an elderly woman across the street making a production of sweeping the sidewalk, though it seemed obvious she was more interested in giving him the once-over.

He tipped the brim of his hat toward her before he started unchaining Greer's car. "Evenin'."

The woman clutched her broom tightly and started across the street. A little black poodle trotted after her. "That's Greer's car," the woman said suspiciously.

He didn't stop what he was doing. "Yes, ma'am."

"What're you doing with it?"

"Unloading it."

She stopped several feet away, still holding the

broom handle as if she was prepared to use it on him if need be. "I don't know you."

"No, ma'am." He fit the wheel ramps in place and hopped up onto the trailer. "I assure you that Greer does." He opened the car door and folded himself down inside it.

Maybe Greer—who was probably all of five two or three without those high heels she was always wearing—could fit comfortably into the car, but he couldn't. Not for any length of time, anyway.

He started the car, backed down the ramp and turned into the driveway. Then he shut off the engine, crawled out from behind the wheel and locked it up again before sticking the key back into the magnetic box he'd found tucked inside the wheel well.

The woman was still standing in the middle of the street.

He secured the ramps back up onto the trailer and gave her another nod. "If you see her, tell her she's got a thermostat problem."

"Tell her yourself." The woman pointed her broom handle at an expensive black SUV that had just crested the top of the hill. "Bet that's her now."

He bit back an oath. He still didn't know what had possessed him to haul Greer's car into town for her, particularly without her knowledge. And his chance of a clean escape had just disappeared.

The SUV pulled to a stop in front of Greer's house. The windows were tinted, so he couldn't see who was behind the wheel, but he definitely could see the shapely leg that emerged when the passenger-side door opened.

It belonged to Greer, looking very un-Greer-like in a flowy sort of dress patterned in vibrant swirls of color that could have rivaled one of his aunt's paintings. Half her hair was untidily pulled up and held by a glittery pink clip.

He still knew it was her, though, and not one of her sisters. No question, considering the sharp look she gave him as she closed the SUV door and approached him. "*You* hauled my car here?"

"I suppose there's no point in denying the obvious." He watched the big SUV pull around in the cul-de-sac and head back down the hill. The identity of the driver was none of his business. He wondered, anyway. "Boyfriend?"

She frowned. "Grant. And why did you haul it?"

No wonder the SUV had turned around and left. "You'd rather have it still sitting out on the side of the highway?"

"Of course not, but—" She broke off, looking consternated, and only then seemed to notice that they had an audience. "How are you doing, Mrs. Gunderson?" She leaned down to pet the little round dog. Ryder wasn't enough of a gentleman to look away when the stretchy, ruffled neckline of Greer's dress revealed more than it should have.

"Just fine, dearie. Oh, Mignon, don't jump!"

Mrs. Gunderson's admonishment was too late, though, because the dog had already bounced up and into Greer's arms.

He was actually a little impressed that the fat Mignon could jump.

But he was more impressed by the way Greer caught him and laughed.

He had never heard her laugh before. Not her or her sisters. Her chocolate-colored eyes sparkled and her face practically glowed.

And damned if he didn't feel something warm streak down his spine.

"You probably need a new thermostat," he said abruptly.

The dog was licking the bottom of her chin even though she was trying to avoid his tongue, but she didn't put Mignon down. "How do you know?"

"Because I checked everything else that would cause your overheating before I towed it back here." He stepped around the two women. "And think about keeping your car key in a less obvious hiding spot," he advised as pulled open the door to climb inside his truck.

Greer's jaw dropped a little, which gave Mignon more chin to lick. She set the dog down and trotted after him, wrapping her fingers over the open window. "You're just going to leave now?"

His fingers closed over the key in the ignition, but didn't turn it. "What else do you figure I should do?"

Her lips parted slightly. "Can I pay you for the tow at least?"

He turned the key. "No need."

"Well, I should do something." She didn't step back from the truck, despite the engine leaping to life. "To thank you at least. Surely there's something I can do."

The "something" that leaped to mind wasn't exactly fit for sharing in polite company. Particularly with her elderly neighbor still watching them as though they were prime-time entertainment.

He said the next best option that came to mind. "Next time I need a lawyer, you can owe me one." He even managed a smile to go with the words.

Fortunately, it seemed like enough. She smiled back and patted the door once. "You'll never collect on that." Her voice was light.

"One thing I've learned in my life is to never say never." He looked away from her ringless ring finger. "Where'd that dog go?"

Greer looked around, giving him a close-up view of the tender skin on the back of her neck. She had a trio of tiny freckles just below the loose strands of hair. Like someone had dashed a few specks of cinnamon across a smooth layer of cream.

He focused on Mrs. Gunderson, who was skirting the back of his trailer, calling the dog's name. "Mignon, get out from under there, right now!"

Greer had joined in, crouching down to look under the vehicle.

He figured if he revved the engine, it might send the fat dog into cardiac arrest. He shut it off again and climbed out. "Where is he?"

"He's lying down right inside the back tire." Mrs. Gunderson looked like she was about to go down on her hands and knees. "Mignon, you naughty little thing. Come out here, right now. Oh, darn it, he seems to have found something he thinks is food."

"Why don't you get one of his usual treats?" Greer suggested.

"Good idea." Mrs. Gunderson set off across the street once more.

If he'd hoped that her departure would spur the dog to follow, he was wrong. He knelt on one knee to look under the trailer. "Come 'ere, pooch."

Mignon paid him no heed at all, except to move even farther beneath the trailer.

Greer crouched next to him. The bottom of her dress puddled around her. "He doesn't like strangers."

Ryder slid his hand out from beneath the soft, colorful fabric that covered it. "He wouldn't like getting flattened by my trailer, either."

"He'll come out for his treats," she assured him.

"Since he looks like he lives on treats, I hope so." It would take the better part of an hour to get home and he'd probably already used up Mrs. Pyle's allotment of patience. If the treat didn't work, he'd have to drag the little bugger out.

"She's actually gotten him to lose a couple pounds."

"He's still wider than he is tall. Reminds me of my aunt's dog, Brutus." He straightened and looked across the street, hoping to see Mrs. Gunderson heading back. Instead, she was just reaching the top of her porch stairs and he could feel the minutes ticking away.

Even though he didn't say anything, Greer could feel the impatience coming off Ryder in waves. She stood, hoping that Mrs. Gunderson moved with more speed than she usually did. It was obvious that he was anxious to be on his way. "Your aunt has an overweight poodle?"

He lifted his hat just long enough to shove his fingers through his thick brown hair. "Overweight pug." His blue gaze slid over her from beneath the hat brim as he pulled it low over his brow. "Adelaide spoils him rotten."

She couldn't help but smile. "A pug named Brutus?"

He shrugged. "She has a particular sense of irony."

"I love your aunt's name," she said. "Adelaide."

A dimple came and went in his lean cheek. "Coming from the woman who lives in that Victorian thing behind us, I'm not real surprised."

She leaned against the side rail of the trailer. "Does she live in New Mexico?" Greer and her sisters didn't know much about Ryder, but had learned that he'd lived in New Mexico before moving to Wyoming.

The brim of his hat dipped slightly. "She has a place near Taos."

"The only place I've ever been in New Mexico was the Albuquerque airport during a layover." She glanced toward her neighbor's house. The front door was still open, but there was no sign of Mrs. Gunderson yet. "Did you grow up there?"

The dimple came again, staying a little longer this time. "In the Albuquerque airport?"

"Ha ha."

His lips actually stretched into a smile. "Yeah. I spent most of my time in Taos."

So she now knew he had an aunt. But she still didn't know if he had parents. Siblings. Other ex-wives. Anybody else at all besides Layla. "What's it like there? It's pretty artsy, isn't it?"

"More so than Braden."

"Does your aunt get to visit you often?"

"She's never been here. She doesn't like to travel much anymore. If I want to see her, I have to go to her." He thumbed up the brim of his hat and squinted at the sky.

"You're anxious to go."

"Yup." He knelt down to look at the dog again. "My housekeeper's gonna be peeved." He gave a coaxing whistle. "Come 'ere, dog."

"Your housekeeper's Doreen Pyle?"

Still down on one knee, he looked up at Greer and something swooped inside her stomach. "Keeping close tabs on me?"

She ignored the strange sensation. "Braden is a small community. And I happen to know her grandson pretty well."

"Dating him, are you?"

She couldn't help the snort of laughter that escaped. "Since he's not legally an adult, hardly. Haven't even had a date in—" She broke off, appalled at herself, embarrassed by the speculative look he was giving her. She pointed, absurdly grateful for Mrs. Gunderson's timely reappearance on her front porch. Her neighbor was holding something in her hand, waving it in the air as she came down the steps. "There's the treat."

And sure enough, before his mistress had even gotten to the street, Mignon was scrabbling out from beneath the trailer, practically rolling over his feet as he bolted.

Ryder straightened and gave her that faint smile again. The one that barely curved his well-shaped lips, but still managed to reveal his dimple. "Never underestimate the power of a good treat."

Then he thumbed the brim of his hat in that way he had of doing. Sort of old-fashioned and, well, *rancherly*. He walked around his truck and climbed inside. A moment later, he'd started the engine and was driving away.

Mrs. Gunderson picked up Mignon, who was happily gnawing on his piece of doggy jerky, and stood next to Greer. "He's a good-looking one, isn't he?"

At least her elderly neighbor could explain away her breathlessness. She'd had to climb her porch stairs to retrieve the dog treats.

Greer, on the other hand, had no such excuse. "He's surprising, anyway." She gave Mignon's head a scratch. "I've got to go call my dad before he drives out to haul my car that no longer needs hauling."

Then she hurried inside, pretending not to hear Mrs. Gunderson's knowing chuckle.

Chapter Three

"Ryder Wilson towed your truck?"

Greer tucked her office phone against her shoulder. "Hey, Maddie. Hold on." She didn't wait for her sister to reply, but clicked over to the other phone call while she scrolled through the emails on her computer. It was Monday morning. She wished she could say it was unusual coming in to find fifty emails all requiring immediate attention. The fact was, coming in to *only* fifty emails was a good start to a week.

"Mrs. Pyle, as I explained to your son last week, Judge Donnelly has refused another continuance in Anthony's case. He's already granted two, which is unusual. Your grandson's trial is going to be on Thursday and my associate Don Chatham will be handling it. He's our senior attorney, as you know, and handles most of the jury trials." After she had handled all the other steps, including negotiating plea deals. Which the prosecutor's office wasn't offering to Anthony this go-round.

Not surprising. It was an election year.

"I know Judge Donnelly." Doreen Pyle sounded tearful. "I can't be in court on Thursday. If I just went to him and asked—"

She shook her head, even though Doreen couldn't see. "I advise you not to speak directly to the judge, Mrs. Pyle."

"Then schedule a different date! You know how unreliable my son is. Anthony needs his family there. If his father would have told me last week, I could have made arrangements. But I have to work!"

Doreen Pyle worked for Ryder Wilson.

Greer pressed her fingertips between her eyes to relieve the pain that had suddenly formed there and sighed. The only adult Anthony truly had in his corner was his grandmother. "I'll see what I can do, Mrs. Pyle. I'll call you later this afternoon. All right?"

"Thank you, Greer. Thank you so much."

She highly doubted that Mrs. Pyle would be thanking her later. "Don't get your hopes up too high," she warned before jabbing the blinking button on her phone to switch back to the other call.

"Sorry about that, Maddie." She sent off a two-line response to the email on her computer screen and started composing a new one to the prosecutor's office. She wouldn't present a motion to the court until the prosecutor agreed to another delay. "You all recovered from the baby shower?"

"The only thing that'll help me recover fully from anything these days will be going into labor. About Ryder—"

"Yes, he towed my truck." She switched the phone to her other shoulder and opened the desk drawer where she kept her active files. "I suppose Ali told you?" She'd caught their father before he'd made a needless trip out to Devil's Crossing but she hadn't told him the finer details of who'd taken care of the chore.

She pulled out the file she was seeking and flipped it open on her desk. Anthony Pyle. Seventeen. Charged with property destruction and defacement. It was his second charge and he was being tried in adult court. Anthony and his grandmother had good cause for worry since he was facing more than six months in jail if convicted.

Greer doubted that his father, Rocky, cared all that much about what happened. He provided for the basic needs of his son, but beyond that, the troubled boy was pretty much on his own. Rocky had told Greer outright that Anthony deserved what he got. Didn't matter to his father at all that the boy had consistently proclaimed his innocence. That the real culprit was his supposed friend—and the son of the man who owned the barn that had nearly burned down.

"Ali? No."

Greer held back a sigh. If Grant had told his wife that he'd seen Ryder with her, there was no way that Ali would have stayed quiet about it. And the fact that Grant hadn't told Ali just meant that he was still conflicted over everything that had happened with his sister.

"You know how news gets around," Maddie said.

In other words, Mrs. Gunderson had told someone she'd seen Ryder towing her car, and that someone had told someone, and so on and so forth.

Greer forestalled her sister's next question, knowing it was coming. "Ryder didn't have Layla with him."

"I heard. Did you know that his latest nanny quit on him?"

Greer's fingers paused on her computer keyboard. Doreen hadn't mentioned *that*. "That's the fourth one."

"Third," Maddie corrected. "Ray has been keeping track."

Greer spotted Keith Gowler in the hallway outside her office and waved to get his attention. He was one of the local private attorneys who took cases on behalf of the public defender's office because they were perpetually overworked and understaffed. "Is Ray concerned?"

"Not that he's said. We have no reason to think Layla's not being properly cared for."

"That's probably why Ryder was anxious to get moving the other evening, then. Doreen must have been watching Layla." And that was why she was upset about not being available for her grandson's trial.

"She's got a lot on her plate, too."

Greer glanced at Anthony's file. Despite the jurisdiction of the case, he was still a minor, which meant the case also involved Maddie's office. "Did you get notice of the trial date?"

"Thursday? Yes. I can't be there, though. Having another ultrasound at the hospital in Weaver and Linc will have kittens if I say I want to reschedule it."

"Everything okay?" she asked, alarm in her voice.

"Everything's fine, except I'm as big as a house and due in two weeks. And don't you start acting as bad as my husband. He's turned into a nervous Nellie these last few weeks. Driving me positively nuts."

"He's concerned. You're having your first baby."

"And I'm already thirty and yada yada. I know."

Keith stuck his head in her doorway. "Got the latest litter?"

She nodded at him and glanced at the round, schoolroom-style clock hanging above the door. It had a loud tick and tended to lose about five minutes every few days, but it had been a gift from one of her favorite law professors what felt like a hundred years ago. "Listen, Maddie, I've got a consult, so I need to go. But I want to know more about the ultrasound. We'll talk—"

"—later," her sister finished and hung up. At least Greer and Maddie were almost always on the same wavelength. It was too bad that Greer couldn't say the same about Ali.

She made a note on her calendar to call her. Maybe if Greer were the one to plan dinner next Monday, she'd get herself back in Ali's good graces. The three of them usually tried to get together for dinner on the first Monday of each month, but their schedules made it difficult. And when it came to canceling, Greer had been the worst offender. The fact that next Monday wasn't the first Monday of the month was immaterial. With Maddie ready to pop with the baby, this might be their only chance for a while.

Keith tossed himself down on the hard chair wedged into Greer's crowded office. "How many assignments this week?"

She closed Anthony's file and plucked a stack from the box on the floor behind her desk. "Too many. Take a look."

"I won't be able to take on as many as usual," he warned as he began flipping through the files. "Lydia and I have set the wedding date next month."

Even though she'd half expected the news, Greer was still surprised. It hadn't been that long since the lawyer was moping around from the supposedly broken heart Ali had caused him when they broke up, before she met Grant. Then he'd met Lydia when he'd taken on the defense case involving her son. "Congratulations. You're really doing it, huh?"

"I'd have married her six months ago, but she wanted to wait until Trevor's case was settled. Now it is and we can get on with our lives." He glanced up for a moment. "How's the Santiago case coming?"

"Pretrial motions after Labor Day. Michael has the investigator working overtime."

"I'll bet he does. Because your boss wants the case dismissed in the worst way."

"We'll see." Stormy Santiago would be the jewel in the prosecutor's reelection crown. She was beautiful. Manipulative. And charged with solicitation of murder. "Don's already prepping to go to trial on it."

"I'll bet he is. He gets her off and he'll be onto bigger pastures, whether he's best buddies with your boss or not. Mark my words."

Greer couldn't imagine Don wanting to leave their department, where he was a big fish in a small pond. "You think?"

Keith shrugged. He slid several folders from the stack toward her. "I can take these."

It was up to her to ensure the assignments were correctly recorded and submitted to the appropriate court clerk. Between municipal, circuit and district courts, it meant even more paperwork for her. "Great. See you in court."

Morning and afternoon sessions were held daily every Monday through Thursday, with Greer running between courtrooms as she handled arraignments and motions and pleadings and the myriad details involved when an individual was charged with a criminal offense. Occasionally, there was a reason for a Friday docket, which was a pain because they all had plenty of non-court details to take care of on Fridays. And increasingly on Saturdays and Sundays, too. Most of those days, Greer was meeting clients—quite often at the various municipal jails scattered around their region.

Such was the life of a public defender. Or in her case, the life of a public defender who got to do all the prep but rarely actually got to *defend*. It was up to Greer to prepare briefs, schedule conferences, take depositions and hunt down reluctant witnesses when she had to. She was the one who negotiated the plea deals that meant Don typically only had to show up in the office on Thursdays, when most of the trials were scheduled. She'd gotten a few bench trials, but thanks to Don and his buddy-buddy relationship with Michael Towers, their boss and the supervising attorney for the region, her experience in front of a jury was limited.

She also photocopied the case files and made the coffee.

But if Don were to ever leave…

She exhaled, pushing the unlikely possibility out of her mind, and sent off her message to the prosecutor. The rest of her email would have to wait. She shoved everything she would likely need into her bulging briefcase, grabbed the blazer that went with her skirt and hurried out of her office.

Michael was sitting behind his desk when she stuck her head in his office. "Any news yet on a new intern?" Their office hadn't had one for three months. Which was one of the reasons Greer had been on coffee and photocopy duty.

He shook his head, looking annoyed. Which for Michael was pretty much the status quo. "I have three other jurisdictions needing interns, too. When there's something you need to know, I'll tell you. Until then, do your job."

She managed not to bare her teeth at him and continued on her way. She didn't stop as she waved at Michael's wife, Bernice, who'd been filling in for the secretary they couldn't afford to hire, even though she hopped up and scurried after her long enough to push a stack of pink message slips into the outer pocket of Greer's briefcase.

"Thanks, Bunny."

Greer left the civic plaza for the short walk to the courthouse. It was handy that the buildings were located within a few blocks of each other. It meant that she could leave her car in the capable hands of her dad for the day. Carter Templeton was retired with too much time on his hands and he'd offered to look at it. He might have spent most of his life in an office as an insurance broker, but there wasn't much that Carter couldn't fix when he wanted to. Which was a good thing for Greer, because she was presently pretty broke.

She was pretty broke almost all of the time.

It was something she'd expected when she'd taken the job with the public defender's office. And money had gotten even tighter when she'd thrown in with her two sisters to buy the fixer-upper Victorian—in which she was the only one still living. She couldn't very well start complaining about it now, though.

The irony was that both Maddie and Ali could now put whatever money they wanted into the house since they'd both married men who could afford to indulge their every little wish.

Now it was just Greer who was holding up the works.

She'd already remodeled her bedroom and bathroom when they'd first moved in. The rest of the house was in a terrible state of disrepair, though. But if she couldn't afford her fair third of the cost, then the work had to wait until she could.

She sidestepped a woman pushing a baby stroller on the sidewalk and jogged up the steps to the courthouse. There were thirty-two of them, in sets of eight. When she'd first started out, running up the steps had left her breathless. Six years later, she barely noticed them.

Inside, she joined the line at security and slid her bare arms into her navy blue blazer. Once through, she jogged up two more full flights of gleaming marble stairs to the third floor.

She slipped into Judge Waters's courtroom with two minutes to spare and was standing at the defendant's table with her files stacked in front of her before the judge entered, wearing his typically dour expression.

He looked over his half glasses. "Oh, goody." His voice was humorless as he took his seat behind the bench. "All of my favorite people are here. Actually on time for once." He poured himself a glass of water and shook out several antacid tablets from the economy-sized bottle sitting beside the water. "All right. As y'all ought to know by now, we'll break at noon and not a minute before. So don't bother asking. If you're not lucky enough to be out of the court's hair by noon, we'll resume at half past one and not one minute after."

He eyed the line of defendants waiting to be arraigned. They sat shoulder to shoulder, crammed into the hardwood bench adjacent to the defendant's table where Greer stood. After this group, there was another waiting, just as large.

Judge Waters shoved the tablets into his mouth. "Let's get started," he said around his crunching.

All in all, it was a pretty normal morning.

* * *

Normal ended at exactly twelve fifty-five.

She knew it, because the big clock on the corner of Braden Bank & Trust was right overhead when she spotted Ryder Wilson walking down the street.

He was carrying Layla.

Greer's heart nearly stopped beating. Heedless of traffic, she bolted across Main Street to intercept him.

A fine idea in theory. But she was wearing high heels and a narrow skirt, and had a ten-pound briefcase banging against her hip with every step she took. Speedy, she was not.

He'd reached the corner and would soon be out of sight.

She'd run track in high school, for God's sake.

She hopped around as she pulled off her pumps, and chased after him barefoot.

The cement was hot under her feet as she rounded the corner and spotted him pulling open the door to Braden Drugs halfway down the block.

"Ryder!"

He hesitated, glancing around over his shoulder, then let go of the door and waited for her.

"Hi!" She was more breathless from the sight of Layla than from the mad dash, and barely looked up at Ryder as she stopped. She knew her smile was too wide but couldn't do a thing about it as she leaned closer to Layla. "Hi, sweetheart. Look at you in your pretty pink sundress. You probably don't even remember me. But I sure remember you."

Layla waved the pink sippy cup by the handle she was clutching and showed off her pearly white teeth as she babbled nonsensically.

Everything inside Greer seized up. She wanted to

take the baby in her arms so badly it hurt. She contented herself with stroking the tot's velvety cheek with her shaking fingertip. "I sure have missed you." The words came out sounding husky, and she cleared her throat before looking up at Ryder.

He was looking back at her warily, which she supposed she deserved, after chasing him down the way she had.

"What brings the two of you to town?"

He looked beyond her to the drugstore. "She's got some special vitamin stuff she's supposed to have. Aren't your feet burning?"

She looked down and felt the searing heat that was only slightly less intense than the heat that filled her cheeks. She quickly leaned over, putting her shoes back on. "Probably looks a little silly."

"Yep."

She huffed. "You didn't have to agree. Do you always say what you're thinking?"

"Not necessarily." His eyebrows quirked. It was her only hint that he was amused. "But I generally say what I mean."

Layla babbled and smacked the sippy cup against Greer's arm. "I think I recognize that cup," Greer said to her.

Layla jabbered back. Her bright green eyes latched onto Greer's.

She felt tears coming on. "I can't believe how much you've grown." The huskiness was back in her voice.

"You want to hold her?"

Now, given the opportunity, Greer was suddenly hesitant. "I don't know if she'll remember me. She might not—"

He dumped the baby in her arms.

Layla smiled brightly. She didn't care in the least that Greer's vision was blurred by tears as she looked down at her.

Greer wrapped her arms around the baby and cuddled her. "I thought she'd be heavier." She closed her eyes and rubbed her cheek against Layla's soft hair. "Nothing smells better," she murmured.

Ryder snorted slightly. "Sure, when she's not fillin' her diaper with something out of a horror flick."

Greer smiled. She caught Layla's fist and kissed it. "What's Daddy talking about, huh, baby? You're too perfect for anything like that."

"Excuse me."

They both looked over to see an elderly woman waiting to enter the door they were blocking.

"Sorry." Greer quickly moved out of the way while Ryder opened the door for her.

The woman beamed at him as she shuffled into the drugstore. "Thank you. It's so nice to see young families spend time together these days."

Greer bit the inside of her cheek, stifling the impulse to correct her. It was the same tactic she'd used many times in the courtroom.

Ryder let the door close after the woman. "Proof that appearances are deceiving."

Greer managed a smile. She was suddenly very aware of the time passing, but she didn't want to look at her watch or give up holding Layla a second sooner than she needed to. "What's special about the vitamins?"

He shrugged. "Something her pediatrician has her taking."

"Do you still take her to my uncle?" David Templeton's pediatrics practice in Braden was older than Greer. He'd been the first one to see Layla when Lincoln had discovered her left on the mansion's doorstep last December.

"You mean he hasn't told you?"

She gave him a look. "Wouldn't be very professional for him to talk about his patients to outsiders. And like it or not, that's what we are these days."

Ryder's lips formed a thin line.

Layla suddenly sighed deeply and plopped her head on Greer's shoulder.

Greer rubbed her back and kissed the top of her head. "I've heard about the nanny problems you've had."

"How?"

She stepped out of the way again when the shop door opened and a woman pushing two toddlers in a stroller came out. "Braden is a small town. Word gets around." She turned slightly so that Layla wasn't positioned directly in the sun. "Nannies don't hold to the same principles of confidentiality that a pediatrician's office does."

His lips twisted. "S'pose not." He reached for Layla, his hands brushing against Greer's bare arms as he lifted the tot away from her.

It was insane to feel suddenly shivery on what was such an infernally hot day.

She adjusted the wide bracelet-style watch on her wrist and wanted to curse. She was late getting back to the courthouse. On foot from here, it would take at least twenty minutes. "I still feel I owe you a favor for helping me this weekend with my car."

"Was it the thermostat?"

"I don't know yet. My dad is looking at it. He's pretty good with cars. I told him what you thought, though." She shifted from one foot to the other and smoothed her hand down the front of her blouse, where it was tucked into the waist of her skirt. He'd taken a step toward the drugstore. "Maybe I could help you on the nanny front," she offered quickly.

"You?" He sounded incredulous. "Kind of a come-down in the world from lawyering to nannying, isn't it?"

"I don't mean *me* personally." She worked hard to keep from sounding as offended as she felt. She might not have a lot of experience with babies, but Layla wasn't just any baby, either. "I mean with advertising for a nanny. I'm on a lot of loops because of my work. I could post ads if you wanted."

His blue eyes gave away none of his thoughts. "I'll think about it."

She took that as a sign he was willing to negotiate. "I've got a lot of connections," she added. "I'd like to help."

Layla's head had found its way to his wide chest and she was contentedly gnawing the handle of her sippy cup.

"I suppose it wouldn't hurt," he said abruptly.

She'd fully expected him to say no. "Great! That's… that's really great." She cringed a little at her overenthusiasm, not to mention her lack of eloquence. She looked at her watch again and quickly leaned forward to kiss Layla's cheek. Then she started backing down the block. "I'll call you later to get the particulars. Pay range, hours, all that."

He resettled his black cowboy hat on his head, looking resigned. "Are you asking or telling?"

She knew her smile was once again too wide, but so what? She'd finally gotten to see Layla. And even if she earned Judge Waters's wrath for not making it back to court on time, she couldn't bring herself to care.

Chapter Four

Ryder spotted the little foreign job sitting in front of his house. It looked as out of place there as it had stalled on the side of the road out near Devil's Crossing.

The second thing he noticed was that Doreen Pyle's ancient pickup truck wasn't there.

When he'd set out that morning to get more hay cut, Mrs. Pyle had been sweeping up cereal after Layla overturned her favorite red bowl.

But now, Mrs. Pyle's truck was gone and the lady lawyer's was parked in its place.

It was too much to hope that she'd come all the way out here to tell him she'd found the perfect nanny candidate. She could've done that over the phone, the same way she'd gotten the particulars from him the other day.

He glanced at the cloudless sky. "What fresh new problem are you giving me now?"

As usual, he got no answer. The air remained hot and heavy, filled with the sound of buzzing insects.

He half expected to find Greer in the kitchen with Layla, but the room was empty when he went in.

He flipped on the faucet and sluiced cold water over his head. Then he grabbed the dish towel hanging off the oven door to mop his face as he went in search of them.

There weren't a lot of rooms in the place, so it didn't take him long. He found both females in the living room, sprawled on his leather couch, sound asleep.

Layla wore a pink sleeveless T-shirt and diaper. She was lying on Greer's chest, who was similarly attired in a sleeveless pink shirt and denim cutoffs.

He looked away from her lightly tanned legs and quietly went up the iron-and-oak staircase. At the top, he crossed the catwalk that bisected the upper back half of the barn. All he had to do was look down and he could see his living area and who was occupying it.

Aside from the failed nannies and Mrs. Pyle, the last woman who'd spent any real time under his roof had been Daisy. When he thought about it, Mrs. Pyle had lasted longest.

He entered his bedroom. He'd put up sliding barn doors in the upper rooms after he'd taken custody of Layla. Before then, the only enclosed spaces had been the bathrooms. Two upstairs. One down.

He went into his bathroom now and flipped on the shower. Dust billowed from his clothes when he stepped out of them. He got into the shower before the water even had a chance to get warm.

He still had goose bumps when he stepped out a few minutes later, but at least he wasn't dripping sweat and covered in hay dust anymore.

He stepped over the dirty clothes, pulled on a pair

of clean jeans and a white T-shirt from his drawer and went back downstairs.

They were still sleeping. He retrieved a bottle of cold water from the fridge in the kitchen, then wearily sat on the only piece of adult-sized furniture in the living room except for the couch. His aunt had designed the armless, triangular-backed chair during her furniture phase, and he had brought it with him along with the couch more for sentimental reasons than because it was comfortable.

He slouched down in the thing as much as he could and propped his bare feet on the arm of the couch by Greer's feet. Instead of opening the water bottle, he pressed it against his head and closed his eyes. Already the relief from the cold shower was waning and he caught himself having fond memories of the three feet of snow piled up against his house last March.

Not two minutes passed before Greer spoke, her voice barely above a whisper. "Do you think the heat's ever going to end?"

He didn't open his eyes. "I spent a summer near Phoenix once." Adelaide had been doing an exhibition there. "I was fifteen." He kept his voice low, too, because he knew what it was like when Layla didn't get in a decent nap. When he'd been rodeoing, he'd drawn broncs that'd been easier to handle. "It was like living inside a pizza oven."

"Descriptive. But you didn't answer my question."

He ignored that. "Where's Mrs. Pyle?"

"Still not answering my question. Obviously, Mrs. Pyle is at her grandson's trial."

He opened his eyes at that. The baby was still sleeping and Greer watched him over her head, eyes as dark and deep as the blackest night.

"What trial?"

"She didn't tell you?"

He spread his hands. "Obviously not."

"You do recall that Doreen Pyle *has* a grandson?"

He gave her a look.

"Anthony's seventeen. And he's being tried for burning down a barn."

Ryder swallowed an oath and pulled his feet off the couch. "She should have told me." He wasn't an ogre. "So why are *you* here?"

"Because I couldn't get the prosecution to agree to another continuance and Judge Donnelly has a stick up his—" Greer broke off with a grimace. "Anthony has a very competent trial lawyer representing him. Today, it's more important for him to have his grandmother there than me."

"Not because you wanted to spend time with Layla?"

"It's the one thing that made today tolerable. I've been working on Anthony's case since his prelim."

"Did he do it?"

"My client is innocent."

"Spoken like a defense lawyer."

"I am a defense lawyer. Just a poorly paid one, thanks to the great state of Wyoming."

"If he's your client, why is someone else handling the trial?"

Her lips twisted. "That, my friend, is the fifty-dollar question." She rolled carefully to one side so that she could deposit Layla on the couch cushion and then slid off the couch to sit on the floor.

It was almost as interesting as watching a circus contortionist.

Once she was on the floor with her back to the couch, she tugged her shirt down over her flat stomach where it had ridden up and blew out a breath. "This place of yours has a lot going for it, I'll grant you, but you need air-conditioning."

"I have a window rattler upstairs in my bedroom." He wondered why he didn't tell her there was another one in Layla's bedroom, too.

She slanted a look toward him from the corner of her eye. "Meaning?"

He smiled slightly. "Meaning I do have air-conditioning. Just not down here. I wish Mrs. Pyle would have told me."

"She must have her reasons. She's known since Monday."

He sat forward and offered her the unopened water bottle. "Why didn't you say something about the trial when you chased us down the street the other day?"

"Because it was Mrs. Pyle's business to tell you." Her fingers grazed his when she leaned over to take the water.

Adelaide had done her best to give him an appreciation of beauty and the visual arts. She'd always been asking him, *But what do you* see? and he never knew exactly what kind of answer she wanted. But he figured he must have learned something from her after all, given his appreciation of the way Greer tilted her head and tipped the bottle back, taking a prolonged drink. Her neck was long and lovely. Her profile pure. Watching her was almost enough to compensate for her and Mrs. Pyle's keeping him in the dark.

Greer handed him back the half-empty bottle.

Her lips were full and damp.

Even though he didn't need the trouble it would likely bring, he didn't look away from her when he took the bottle from her and finished it.

Her gaze flickered and she looked away as she pushed to her feet. She tugged at the hem of her T-shirt as she paced around the couch. "Did she give you any other reason to be quitting?"

"Maybe you should ask Mrs. Pyle."

She gave him a look and he relented, proving that he needed more willpower to resist the women in his life. "She tells me she's a housekeeper. Not a nanny."

"Because scrubbing floors is so much easier than heating a bottle?" Her voice rose a little and she pressed her lips together self-consciously.

"Layla doesn't use a bottle anymore. She only uses her cup. The pink cup. And if the pink cup isn't handy, she screams bloody murder until it is. Trust me, Counselor. Cleaning house is easier than childcare." He waved at Layla, who hadn't budged an inch from where she had rolled onto her side against the back couch cushion. She drooled all the time these days, and now was no exception. But the leather had survived him growing up, so he assumed it would survive a while longer.

"Did she say when she's leaving?"

"She gave me a week's notice."

"Even if we haven't found a nanny by then?" Greer propped her hands on her slender hips. "Did she say anything else?"

"Yeah. That I'd be better off finding a wife than a nanny."

Greer's eyebrows rose halfway up her forehead. Then she scrubbed her hands down her face. "I'm sorry."

"For what?"

She dropped her hands. "That she said something so…so insensitive!" She pressed her lips together again and watched Layla warily, as if expecting her to wake because her voice had risen once more.

"Insensitive how?"

A small line formed between her eyebrows. "Your wife passed away less than a year ago," she said huskily. "I'm sure remarrying is the furthest thing from your mind."

"It was until my housekeeper brought it up. But she had a valid point. Layla deserves a mother." At least he'd had Adelaide when his mother had died. He leaned back in the chair again and propped his feet once more on the couch arm. He linked his fingers across his stomach. "You never knew Daisy, did you?"

The line deepened slightly as she shook her head. "I never met her. But Grant has been talking more about Karen these days."

"The man actually talks?"

She gave him a look. "What she did has been hard on him, too. He was Karen's brother, but even then, the court wasn't ready or willing to hand over Layla to him."

He grunted. "She was never Karen to me. She was Daisy Miranda. That was the name she used when we met, the name she used when we got married and the name she used when she left me. She never said she had a brother at all. Either he didn't matter enough for her to mention, or I didn't matter enough. Considering the way things went down, I'll give you a guess which one I'm more inclined to believe."

Greer tucked her hair behind her ears. Her forehead had a dewy sheen. "Regardless of her name, you loved her enough to marry her. You don't just get over that at the drop of a hat."

"You been married to someone who ran out on you? Ever gone through a bunch of tests just to make sure she didn't leave you with something catching to remember her by?"

"No, but—"

"Ever married at all?"

She needlessly retucked her hair. "No. But that doesn't mean I don't have feelings. That I have no appreciation for the pain involved when you lose someone. Hearts don't heal just because we decide they should."

He couldn't help the amusement that hit him.

And she saw it on his face. The line between her brows deepened even more. "What's so funny?"

He schooled his expression. "Nothing."

She let out a disgusted sound and his lips twitched again. Stopping the smile would've taken more willpower than he possessed.

She glared at him even harder and her eye got that little twitch she was prone to.

"Relax, Counselor. You don't have to worry that I'm withering away with grief or anything else because of my beloved wife. You do recall that *she* ran out on me, right?"

"And no matter what you say now, I'm sure that was very painful for you. But you know—" she waved her hands in invitation "—if you feel the need to pretend otherwise so as to maintain some false manly pride, be my guest."

He watched her for a moment. Then he pulled his feet off the couch again and sat forward. "Want a beer?"

She blinked. "What?"

He stood. Layla was still sound asleep. Snoring even, which meant that although he'd showered off the hay dust, she'd still probably gotten a whiff of it and her nose was getting congested. The pediatrician had warned him that Layla seemed to be developing some allergies. "A beer," he repeated, and headed into the kitchen, where he grabbed two cold bottles from the refrigerator.

Greer was standing in the same spot when he returned and handed her one. "It's five o'clock somewhere." He twisted off the cap and set it on the fireplace mantel.

Still looking suspicious, she slowly did the same.

He lightly tapped his bottle against hers and took a drink.

After some hesitation, she took a tiny sip.

"Let's go out back. It might be cooler."

She looked at Layla. "But—"

He scooped up the baby, who didn't even startle, and transferred her to the playpen. Then he picked up the baby monitor and turned it on, showing Greer the screen where the black-and-white image of his living space, including the playpen, was flickering to life. "Happy?"

Beer and monitor in hand, he headed out through the kitchen door, and Greer followed.

It wasn't any cooler outside. But at least there was a slight breeze and the gambrel roof provided shade from the sun. He gestured with his bottle to the picnic table and benches that he'd found stored in the root cellar when he'd bought the place.

"Wouldn't have expected something so fanciful from you," she said as she straddled one of the benches and set her bottle on the cheerfully painted table. "Flowers?"

He took the opposite bench. "Daisies." He set the baby monitor on the center of the weathered table and took a pull on the cold beer. "Twenty-five cents if you can guess who painted them."

"Ah." She nodded and fell silent.

He exhaled and turned so his back was against the table and he could stretch out his legs. The rolling hillside was his for almost as far as he could see. Beyond that was his by lease. His closest neighbor was ten miles away as the crow flew, and just to get to the highway meant driving down his seventeen-mile driveway, three miles of which were actually paved. Until he'd bought the place, he felt like he'd been looking for it his entire life.

But his housekeeper did have a point about his place being remote. "Mrs. Pyle's grandson going to get off?"

"It's a jury trial, so you never know until the verdict comes in. But I believe the facts are on Anthony's side."

"Doesn't it bug you not being there in court?"

"There are a lot of things about my job that bug me." He took another drink and looked her way.

"Yes. It bugs me. But we've built a solid defense and Don Chatham—much as he annoys me personally—is a fine attorney. I can zealously represent my clients through the fairest plea negotiations to resolve their cases as well as anyone working in the PD's office. But when my client refuses to plea, or when they're truly better served going to trial?" She rolled the bottle between her fingertips. "Anthony *is* in good hands. Better than mine, when it comes down to it, since Don's experience before a jury exceeds mine by about a decade."

"When's the verdict likely to come in?"

"Before six tonight. The judge runs a tight ship and he likes to be home for dinner with his wife every night by seven. If the jury is still deliberating, he'll call a recess and resume tomorrow morning. But he'll be in a bad mood because he doesn't like working on Fridays any more than Don does. Did you move here because of Daisy?"

Her abrupt question was surprising. "No. We didn't meet until after that." He rolled his jaw around. "Not long after," he allowed.

"So why did you buy this place? Did you ranch in New Mexico?"

"I did a lot of ranch work. For other people. Along the way was some rodeoing. A few years in the service. Did you always want to be a lawyer?"

"What branch?"

"Army."

She smiled slightly. "My dad, too. Way before I was born, though." Her smile widened. "And I wanted to be a lawyer from the very first Perry Mason novel I read. My dad has a whole collection of them from when he was a kid and I started reading them one summer when I was grounded. I had romantic visions of defending the rights of the meek and the defenseless. And I also fancied following in Archer's path."

Ryder lifted his eyebrows.

"My older brother. Half brother, to be accurate. On my dad's side. I have a half sister on my mom's side who's also an attorney. But I didn't grow up with Rosalind the way I did with Archer. They're both in private practice."

"Classic yours, mine and ours situation?"

"Sort of. I have another half sister, too, who is a psychologist. Hayley lives in Weaver with her husband, Seth, and their baby. What about you?"

"No sisters. No brothers. Half or otherwise."

"But you have an aunt Adelaide with a pug named Brutus."

"Lawyers and their penchant for details."

"I'd be worried about my memory if I couldn't recall something you mentioned less than a week ago," she said drily. "What about your parents?"

"What about them?"

She waited a beat, and when he said nothing more,

she took a sip of her beer. She squinted and her cheeks looked pinched.

Her face was an open book, which for a lawyer was sort of a surprise. Maybe it was a good thing she didn't face juries very often. "Not your cup of tea?"

"It's fine."

He rolled his eyes and took the beer out of her hands. "I suppose you're a teetotaler."

"Not at all. I just… Well, wine is more my thing."

It was his turn to pull a face. "And not mine. Whiskey?"

"If the occasion calls for it."

"We've at least got that in common." He got up and she looked alarmed. "Don't worry. I'm not bringing out a bottle of the good stuff. A cold beer at three on a hot afternoon is one thing. We'll save the whiskey for cold nights and staying warm. I'll get you a soda."

Greer chewed the inside of her cheek, watching Ryder head inside his house.

She thought she'd done pretty well not falling right off the couch when she'd wakened to find him sitting there. He'd obviously showered. His hair was dark and wet, slicked back from his chiseled features. His T-shirt was clinging to his broad shoulders. His feet sticking out from the bottom of his worn jeans had been bare.

And her mind had gone straight down the no-entry road paved with impossibility.

She hadn't expected to doze off along with Layla. But then again, she hadn't expected to be so pooped out after spending six hours taking care of the baby, either.

When she'd arrived out at the house, it had been early enough to relieve Doreen Pyle so she could get into town before court started. But Ryder hadn't been there, even though Greer had spent most of last night sleeplessly preparing herself for the encounter.

Doreen had told her that he'd headed out more than two hours earlier. "Haying," she'd said, as if that explained everything.

Foolishly, Greer had assumed that Doreen would have told her employer that Greer was pinch-hitting that day. And why.

She turned the baby monitor so she could see it better. Layla had turned around in a full circle inside the playpen, but still looked to be sleeping.

She reluctantly set the monitor on the table when Ryder returned. He set a bottle of cola in front of her. "Better?"

She rarely indulged, but it was still better than beer. And it was wonderfully cold. "Thank you."

His lips stretched into a brief smile. Then he sat down again, but this time he straddled his bench the same as her. "Why choose the public defender's office to zealously defend your clients?"

She'd been asked that question ever since she'd passed the bar. She'd always given the same answer. "Because I wanted to help people who really needed it." Her eyes strayed to the baby monitor. She couldn't help it. That grainy little image fascinated her.

"And do you?" His question dragged at her attention. "Help people who really need it?"

She twisted open the soda and took a long drink. The fact that she wasn't really sure what she was accomplishing anymore wasn't something she intended to share. "Everyone deserves a proper and fair defense," she finally said, which she believed right to her very core. "More than eighty percent of criminal defendants in this state end up in the public defender's office. I do my part as well as I can."

"Just not in front of a jury."

She realized she'd picked up the monitor again and made herself put it down. "Not generally. Although, honestly, I stay busier with my cases than Don does. We have a handful of trials a month. Unless it's something really big like the Santiago thing that's been on the news, Don spends most of his weekends fishing while I'm chasing around between courts and jails and—" She broke off. "I've never had a caseload that drops under one hundred clients at any given time."

The slashing dimple in his cheek appeared for a moment. "Do they all say they're innocent?"

She smiled wryly and let that one pass. "We cover a few counties here. But I know some offices with caseloads that are even heavier. We all make use of interns, but getting them can be sort of cutthroat." She shook her head. "The real problem is there's never enough money in the coffers to equip our office with everything and everyone we need."

"Now you sound like a politician."

On the monitor screen, Layla had turned around and was facing the other corner, her little rump up in the air. "Not in this lifetime," Greer responded. "Though I'd probably make more money if I were. Nobody I know has ever gotten rich working as a PD."

"Do you want to be rich?"

She laughed outright at that. "I'm more about being able to pay all the bills on time."

"What about that house of yours? That's gotta be a money pit."

"I'll take the fifth on that. I love my house. It has character."

"Like your car?"

She gave him her best stern look. The one she'd learned from her father. "Don't be dissing my car."

He lifted his hands in surrender.

"It *was* the thermostat, by the way. So thank you for that heads-up."

"Ever considered private practice?"

"Most lawyers do."

"Well, then? It's not like you don't have an in with people in the business."

"Much as I love Archer, I have no desire to actually *work* with him. Rosalind is with *her* father's practice down in Cheyenne and does mostly tax and corporate law. Bo-ho-ring. So—" She took another drink just so she wouldn't pick up the monitor again.

"So…?"

"Why are you so interested?"

"Shouldn't I know more about the woman who's been watching Layla behind my back?"

"For one day. Don't imply it's been a regular occurrence." She nudged the monitor with her fingertip. "We all fell in love with her, you know." She brushed her thumb across Layla's black-and-white image. "Right from the very beginning when Linc called in Maddie because he'd found a baby on his doorstep. The only identifying clue she had on her was the note Daisy left with her."

"'Jaxie, please take care of Layla for me,'" he recited evenly.

"Right. When Daisy cocktailed for Jax at his bar, she routinely called him that. That's the only reason we ever suspected she was Layla's mother in the first place."

Ryder's expression was inscrutable but she could easily imagine what his suspicions were. She'd had them herself. So had Linc. His brother, Jax, had been on one of his not-infrequent jaunts, which was why Linc hadn't immediately turned over the baby when he first discovered her. But whether or not Jax had been involved with Daisy in a more personal way, they'd nevertheless conclusively ruled him out as the baby's biological father last December.

She set the monitor down again. "By the time we knew about Daisy, though, Layla was already under the court's protection. The judge named Maddie as Layla's emergency foster parent while an investigation began." She was reiterating facts that he'd been told months ago.

"Your sister and Linc wanted to adopt her themselves. Before you ever even knew Daisy's brother existed."

She glanced at him. It wasn't a detail they'd shared when he took custody. "Who told you that?"

He swirled the liquid in his bottle and took a drink, making her wonder if he was stalling or if he was simply thirsty.

Then he turned the bottle upside down and poured out the remaining beer onto the grass beneath their feet. "Not cold enough," he said, and she thought he wasn't going to answer her at all.

But he surprised her.

He laid the empty bottle on its side on the table between them and slowly spun it. "As you've pointed out before, Counselor, word gets around in a small town." He stopped the bottle so it pointed her way. "Isn't it true?"

She was a lawyer. Not a liar. And what was the harm if he knew the truth now? Maybe if he really understood, he wouldn't be so standoffish where her family and Layla was concerned. "They would have, but

Maddie knew she and Linc would never get her. There were too many people in line ahead of them waiting to adopt a baby."

She clasped her hands on the table in front of her before she could pick up the monitor again. Her fascination with it was vaguely alarming. "The search for Daisy was leading nowhere and it was only a matter of time before Judge Stokes made a permanent ruling about placement. Not even the fact that Ali found Daisy's brother and discovered her real name was Karen Cooper changed that. We couldn't prove Layla was Karen's daughter and Grant's niece through his DNA because both he and Karen were adopted. Siblings by law, but not by genetics. Which meant that not even Grant could stop the legal forces at work. The one established fact the court recognized was that Layla had been abandoned and, as such, would benefit from placement in a suitable home through adoption. A family had even been selected." She sneaked a look at Ryder's face but his expression still told her nothing. She spread her fingers slightly, then pressed the tips of her thumbs together. "And then we discovered that your...that Karen had died in a car accident in Minnesota. Thanks to the photo that Grant and Ali found in her effects, we learned about you. Until then, we had no idea that Daisy Miranda or Karen Cooper had acquired a husband."

"The presumptive father, you mean."

She studied him. He'd had an opportunity to disprove it simply by requesting a paternity test.

But he hadn't.

Instead, he'd admitted—under oath—that he'd known about his absent wife's pregnancy. Combined with all their other information about Karen Cooper, it was enough for Judge Stokes to determine that Layla was

legally Ryder's child. She'd been born during their marriage. No further questions asked. Certainly not about
why Karen hadn't left their child with Ryder when she'd
apparently decided parenthood wasn't for her.

The case may have been closed, but that didn't mean
there weren't still questions.

"You didn't have to do it, you know," she said after
a moment. "Claim Layla as your child. Not when we'd
already failed so spectacularly to prove maternity." She
didn't want to know if he'd lied under oath. It was hard
enough suspecting that he had.

"It was the right thing to do."

"Even though *we* didn't know for certain that Daisy
is…was Layla's mother." She could think of a dozen clients who wouldn't have done what he'd done. He'd told
Ali when they'd first notified him that his wife hadn't
been pregnant when she'd left him. Yet when he'd appeared before Judge Stokes, he'd attested that Daisy
had notified him.

"How often do you run into someone named Layla?"
He didn't wait for an answer as he spun the bottle again.
"It was my mother's name. Daisy knew it. And I know
Daisy liked it, because she told me once—in the beginning when I thought we actually had something—that if
we ever had a baby girl, she wanted to name her Layla.
Daisy *was* Layla's mother." He dropped his hand onto
the bottle again, stopping its spinning once more. "It
was the right thing to do," he repeated after a moment.

Greer's chest squeezed. He believed Daisy was Layla's
real mother. But did he believe that Layla was his biological daughter?

She reached across the table and covered both his
hand and the bottle with hers. "I'm sorry, Ryder. I really
am." That he lost his wife. That he'd become a father in

such an unconventional way. If she had questions, he surely had many more.

His jaw canted to one side. Then his blue eyes met hers and for some reason, an oil slick of panic formed inside her. She started to pull her hand back, but he turned his palm upward and caught hers.

"Sorry enough to marry me?"

Chapter Five

"*Marry you?*"

Greer yanked on her hand and nearly fell off the
bench when he let go of it. She caught herself, only to
knock over the bottle of soda, which gushed out in a
stream of bubbly foam, splashing over the front of her
T-shirt and shorts. "Now look what you've done!"

It was obvious he was having a hard time not laughing. "Gonna sue me over it? You know, for a woman
who looks like she can run the world, you're kind of a
klutz. Did you really think I was serious?"

She plucked her wet shirt away from her belly. Now
she wasn't just sweaty, she'd be sticky, too. And she'd
never been klutzy. Until she was around him. "Of
course not," she lied. "You're just full of funny things
to say this after—" She broke off when he suddenly
stood and went inside the house.

She muttered an oath after his departing backside
and swiped her hand down her wet thighs.

He returned a moment later, holding a sleepy-looking Layla and a checkered dish towel that he tossed Greer's way. "She needs a fresh diaper."

"Am I supposed to take out an announcement in the newspaper?" She swiped the towel over her legs. She could feel the damn soda right through to the crotch of her cutoffs.

"You're pretty snarky when you're caught off guard, aren't you?" He went back inside.

Then she realized the baby monitor had gotten doused with soda, too. She snatched it off the table and started drying it with the towel.

The screen had gone black.

She carried it inside. Ryder was bending over Layla on the couch, changing the diaper. "Do you have any dried rice?" She didn't wait for an answer, but started opening cupboard doors. "Ali got her cell phone wet last year and kept it inside a container of rice for a day to dry. I had my doubts, but the thing worked afterward." Greer found plates. Drinking glasses. At least a dozen boxes of dry cereal. Only half of it was suitable for Layla, which gave her quite the insight into his preference for Froot Loops.

She moved on to the lower cabinets and drawers.

"No, I do not have rice."

He spoke from right behind her and she straightened like he'd poked her with an electric prod. "Oh." She slammed the drawer she'd just opened shut. "Well, then I don't know what you'll want to do about this." She set the monitor on the butcher-block counter. "More soda got on it than me."

He lifted an eyebrow as he settled Layla into the high chair and managed to fasten the little belt thing around her wriggling body. "You look pretty soaked."

It was all she could do not to pluck at the hem of her shorts. "Yeah, well, you shouldn't joke like that."

He slid the molded tray onto the high chair and grabbed one of the boxes of cereal. He dumped a healthy helping onto Layla's tray and she dived into it like she hadn't eaten in days.

There was no question that Layla liked her food. Greer had fed her both jars of the food that Doreen had left out, plus a cubed banana and a teething biscuit, right before her nap.

"Yeah, well, maybe I shouldn't be joking. Mrs. Pyle's the one who reminded me Layla'd be better off with a mama than a nanny. Not that I've had any luck keeping either one around," he added darkly.

She felt that slick panic again and opened her mouth to say something, but nothing came. Which was such an unfamiliar occurrence that she felt even more panicky. "You can't judge everyone based on Daisy and a flighty nanny," she finally managed to say.

"Three nannies," he reminded her. "Easier to discount one two-week wife than three nannies. Mrs. Pyle had a point."

She wasn't sure her eyebrows were ever going to come back down to their normal spot over her eyes. "On what planet?"

He slid a look her way. "I know I'm not Wyoming's biggest catch, but you really think I can't find a wife if I set my mind on it? At least this time, I'd be choosing with my head instead of my—"

"Heart?"

His lips twisted. "That wasn't exactly the body part I was thinking about."

She felt her cheeks heat, which was just ridiculous. It wasn't as though she was some innocent virgin. She was well versed in the facts of life, whether or not she'd acted on any of those facts lately.

"Anyway," he went on, "it wouldn't be a one-way deal." He'd pulled a covered bowl from the refrigerator and dumped the contents in a saucepan that he set over a flame on the stove. "I realize that she'd need to get something out of it, too. It'd be a business deal." He bent over, picking up the sippy cup that Layla had pitched to the floor. "Both parties benefit."

Greer nearly choked, looking away from the sight of his very, very fine jean-clad backside.

He set the cup back on the tray. "If you throw it, I'm going to take it away," he warned.

The baby laughed and swept her hands back and forth against the cereal, sending pieces shooting off the tray.

"Yeah, you laugh, you little terror," he muttered. "You know better." He went back to the stove to poke a fork at the concoction he was heating.

It all felt strangely surreal.

"I've always been better in business than relationships. So go with your strengths, right?" He glanced at her again.

"Marriage isn't a business deal."

He snorted. "Better a business deal than the real deal. As they say, Counselor, been there, done that. Not really a fan. You've been a lawyer for a while now. Haven't you seen the value of pragmatism over idealism?"

She wanted to deny it, but couldn't. "I don't think pragmatism is a basis for marriage, either."

"But it's a good basis for good business. At least that's been my experience. So—" he tested the temperature of the contents in his saucepan with his finger and pulled the pan off the flame "—like I said, Mrs.

Pyle has a point. Two parents are supposed to be better than one. Didn't have two, myself, so I don't know about that. Maybe if I had—" He broke off, shaking his head and leaving Greer wondering.

He tipped the saucepan over a small bowl and grabbed a child-sized spoon from a drawer before flipping one of the table chairs around to face the high chair. "Every kid deserves a mother. Don't you agree?"

"Yes, but that doesn't mean I agree with this method of acquiring one!"

"People have been marrying for practical reasons a lot longer than they've been marrying for romantic ones. I could advertise for a wife just as easily as I can a nanny."

"You know what this sounds like to me? Like you've put all of five minutes of thought into it."

"And you'd be wrong. What happens to Layla if something happens to me?"

Her lips parted. "You… Well, Grant—"

"Daisy didn't dump Layla on Grant's doorstep. You think that was just an oversight? She didn't want him to have her!"

"You can't blame him for that! She didn't leave Layla with you, either!"

"Yeah, and that's something I get to live with. Daisy still named her after *my* mother. She was as unpredictable as the wind, but that means something to me."

She exhaled, feeling a pang inside. "Ryder. We'll find you a nanny. One who'll stay."

"If you were a kid, would you rather have a mom or a paid babysitter?" He didn't wait for her to answer. "Putting that aside for the moment, I'd rather have another plan in place for Layla if I get stomped out by a pissed-off bull one day."

"I've got to sit down." She grabbed one of the wood chairs from the table and sank down onto it. "I'm a lawyer. I appreciate your wisdom in planning for disasters, but I don't particularly want that vision in my head."

"You've heard worse in court, I'm sure."

She had, but that was different. "You can name anyone you want as a guardian for Layla if something were to happen to you. For heaven's sake, if you want to write up a will right now, I can help you. It doesn't mean you have to have a business-deal wife."

"Fine." He gestured with the spoon. "There's paper in that drawer. Get out a piece."

She slid open the drawer in question and pulled out the notepad and a short stub of a pencil. "You don't have to do it this very second."

"No time like the present." He scooped food into Layla's mouth.

"Maybe you should give it more thought," she suggested. "Deciding who would best—"

"I, Ryder Wilson, being of sound mind and body, yada yada. I assume you can fill in the blanks."

She exhaled noisily. "I'm not so sure about the soundness," she muttered. "But yes. So who do you want to name as guardian? Your aunt Adelaide?"

"She's already done her time raising me. You."

"Me, what?"

"You. Put your name down."

She dropped the pencil back into the drawer and shut it with a snap. "I don't find this funny."

"I don't find it funny, either, Counselor. There's no denying you've got a strong concern for Layla. But if your concern isn't that strong, no sweat." He scooped up another spoonful of the unidentifiable substance and evaded Layla's grasping hands to shovel it into her greedy mouth.

Something about his actions made Greer's insides feel wobbly. So she focused instead on the goopy little chunks on the spoon. "What *is* that?"

"Sweet potatoes, beets and ground chicken."

"Good grief."

"Don't knock it. I call it CPS."

"What?"

"Cow Pie Surprise."

She grimaced. "You just said it was chicken."

"It is. But doesn't matter what meat I add, it all looks the same. Like Cow Pie Surprise. But Layla loves it and she's sleeping better at night since I started spiking her food with meat." He gave Greer a sideways look. "You're not vegetarian or something, are you?"

She shook her head, keeping silent about her brief stint with the practice during her college years.

"Good." He focused back on Layla, slipping in a couple more bites before she managed to commandeer the spoon and whack it against the side of the tray. She chattered indecipherably, occasionally stopping long enough to focus on drumming her spoon or carefully choosing a round piece of cereal.

He tossed the bowl in the sink and wet a cloth to start wiping up the mess that was all over Layla's face and hands and hair and tray and clothes.

"Don't you have a bib?"

"Couple dozen of 'em. All came in the boxes of stuff your sister sent. Short-Stuff here doesn't like 'em." He freed the baby and set her down on the floor, and she immediately started crawling out of the room. "Decided a while ago that it wasn't worth the battle."

Having spent much of the day keeping up with Layla,

Greer was less surprised by the rapid crawl than she was by Ryder's ease with Layla. She'd pictured him as struggling a bit more with the day-to-day needs of a baby.

"Do you have other children?"

His eyes narrowed and Greer knew she'd annoyed him. "D'you see any other kids here?"

She scooped up Layla before the baby could get too far. "Don't be so touchy." She much preferred taking the offensive tack to being on the defensive. "Nanny problems or not, you've obviously settled into the routine."

"Better than you expected."

"Not at all." *Liar, liar, pants on fire.*

"I've got roundup facing me whether this heat breaks soon or not, and it'll mean being gone a couple days. No matter what you think it looks like, I still need help. Nanny, wife or otherwise."

"And I'll remind you yet again that I have an entire family willing to help you out where Layla is concerned."

"Like Maddie? Your sister who is so pregnant she looks like she's about ready to explode?"

"How do you know what she looks like?"

"She was in Josephine's diner the other day."

"She didn't mention seeing you."

"She didn't."

He didn't elaborate, and Greer stomped on her impatience as though she were putting out a fire.

"I've already made some job postings for another nanny. It's only a matter of time before you find the right person. Here." She handed Layla to him. "I have briefs I need to prepare." She'd even brought her case files with her, thinking she might have time to make some notes while Layla napped. But since Greer had napped right along with her, clearly *that* had been a silly notion. And even though she did have work to do, it was the sudden need to escape from Ryder that was driving her now.

"Briefs for a job that's not everything you'd hoped for."

"I didn't say that."

"You didn't have to." His gaze pinned hers and she felt uncomfortably like a witness about to perjure herself before the court.

She dragged her soda-moist shirt down around her soda-moist shorts. "I'll let you know when there are a few candidates—*nanny* candidates—for you to interview." She waved her hand carelessly. "But by all means, don't let that stop you from putting out word that you're wife-hunting if you're actually serious about that."

"Maybe I'll do that."

"If you do, I hope you'll look beyond the pool of cocktail waitresses at Magic Jax." The second she said it, she felt terrible. "I'm sorry. That was in poor taste."

"At least it was honest. You can let me know if you want to toss your name in the pool, after all."

She wasn't falling for that again. She snatched up her purse and her briefcase where she'd stashed them out of Layla's reach and hurried to the front door. "I'll be in touch about your will." She didn't wait for a response as she stepped outside and yanked the door closed.

She stood still for a moment and exhaled shakily. It was that time of day when the sun cast its rays beneath the covered front porch. It shone over her shoes. Her legs.

Marry Ryder.

She blinked several times, trying to ignore the words whispering through her mind.

Marry Ryder.

Try as she might, the thought would not be ignored.

"Get real," she whispered. He'd been no more serious about that than he had about naming her as Layla's
guardian in his will. She stepped off the porch and
strode decisively toward the car.

Marry.

Ryder.

Greer heard the front door open. "In the kitchen," she
yelled, where she was putting the final touches on the
tray of cold veggies and fruit. The heavens had finally
smiled on her and her sisters' calendars, and Monday
dinner was actually under way. She picked up the tray
and carried it into the living room, where Maddie was
struggling to lower herself onto the couch.

"Hold on. I'll help you." She set the tray on the coffee table, but Maddie waved her off.

"It's so hot," she grumbled, pushing her dark hair
off her forehead.

"I've got lemonade or iced tea ready."

"Can you throw in some vodka?" Maddie made a
face when Greer hesitated. "I'm joking." Even though
she'd just sat, she pushed to her feet again and rubbed
the small of her back. "Maybe."

The door opened and Ali blew in. "Have you heard
Vivian's latest?"

Greer met Maddie's gaze before they both warily
looked toward their sister. Where their paternal grandmother was concerned, anything was possible. Vivian
Archer Templeton was nothing if not eccentric. And the
fact that she was enormously wealthy thanks to Penn-
sylvania steel and several dead husbands meant she usu-

ally had no obstacles standing in the way of exercising those eccentricities.

"No," Maddie said cautiously. "What's she done now?"

"She went out on a *date* with Tom Hook!"

Greer stared. Tom Hook was an attorney. And a rancher. And a good twenty years younger than their eighty-ish grandmother. "Are you sure it was a date?"

Maddie let out a wry laugh. "Better a date than a marriage."

True enough. Their grandmother had already buried four husbands. "Vivian's always saying she has no interest in another husband because she's already had the love of her life in dear Arthur," Greer needlessly reminded them. He'd been the fourth of their grandmother's husbands. The only one who hadn't been rich. And Vivian made no secret of the fact that she would be happy to join him whenever the good Lord saw fit. After a life riddled with mistakes for which she'd been trying to make amends during the last few years, she maintained that Arthur was the one thing she ever did completely right.

"I'm guessing she's not looking for the love of her life," Ali said drily as she dropped her keys on the little table by the stairs. "Maybe she just wants some male companionship." She wiggled her eyebrows, looking devilish.

Greer made a face. "Don't be gross, baby sister."

Instead of getting Ali's goat, the reminder that she was the youngest of the triplets just made her laugh. "I'm a married woman now," she retorted, waggling her wedding rings. "Maybe I *like* thinking that I'll still be interested in that sort of thing when I'm Vivian's age."

"I'm even less eager to hear about your sex life than Vivian's."

Ali's eyes were merry. "Admit it, Greer. You're jealous. You need a date way worse than Vivian."

She rolled her eyes, ignoring the accusation that was too close to the truth. "So we can suspect why Vivian's dating Tom, but what's Tom up to?"

"Greer," Maddie chided. "Vivian's an intelligent, stylish woman."

"She's loaded," Ali said, ever blunt.

"Tom's not seeing her for her money," Maddie argued. "It doesn't jibe with his personality at all. He's a good guy. Tell her I'm right, Greer."

"He's a good attorney," Greer allowed. "I always thought he had a lot of common sense. But to date Vivian? I don't know about that." She was as fond of their eccentric grandmother as her sisters were, but Tom and Vivian dating? "What if he's after her money?"

"You think if he were that she's too feeble to know?" Ali smiled wryly. "Fact is, *he's* the one we should probably be worried about. Vivian's pretty wily."

"It's just a date!" Maddie objected. "It's certainly not the craziest thing that's ever happened around here. And it doesn't have to mean marriage is afoot." She was still rubbing her back as she waddled into the kitchen. "Even for Vivian."

"Watch out for the two loose floorboards," Greer called out to her. What would her sisters say if she told them about Ryder's ridiculous wife idea? "I put a chair over them."

Maddie reappeared in the doorway. She was carrying a second tray and her cheek bulged out like a chipmunk's. "I wondered why it was sitting in the middle of the room," she said around her mouthful of food.

She bent her knees enough so that she could slide the tray of cheese and crackers onto the coffee table without spilling the contents, then worked her way back down onto the couch. "When did we start having loose floorboards?"

"When did we not have them?" Ali responded. She sat down in the chair across from Maddie and pulled the trays closer, selecting a cluster of fat red grapes. "Are we having anything hot, or just cold stuff?"

"Just cold." Greer grabbed a fresh strawberry from the tray. "I have cold cuts and rolls, too, if you're interested."

"Much as I love sandwiches, it's too dang hot." Ali propped her sandaled feet on the edge of the couch. "Heard your esteemed colleague got Anthony Pyle off in court last week." She dangled her grapes in the air before plucking one from the stem. "Must feel good to know your department has put another little punk back on the streets."

Greer's nerves tightened. Anthony's verdict hadn't come in until evening on the day that she'd babysat Layla. But instead of being in the courthouse as she should have been, she'd been pacing around her house trying to forget everything that Ryder had said. "It does feel good. Particularly since your department neglected to arrest the right person in the first place."

"Come on," Maddie said tiredly. "No arguments about work, okay?" She winced a little and rubbed her hand over her massive belly.

Greer peered at her. "When are you going to start your maternity leave from Family Services?"

"End of the week. I'm not due until next week, of course, but it's just starting to be too hard to get through—"

"—the doorways?"

Maddie elbowed Ali. "Ha ha. Soon enough you'll be in the same fix." She looked back at Greer. "The days," she finished. "Linc's been on my case to stop working for the past month, and my obstetrician for the past two weeks. Arguing with them both is too much work when—" She winced again and blew out a long breath.

"When you're this close to popping," Ali interjected. She closed her hand over Maddie's and squeezed. "You know you don't have to justify anything to us."

"Ali's right." Greer sat on the arm of the couch next to their pregnant sister. She rubbed Maddie's shoulder, left bare by the loose, sleeveless sundress she wore. "I'm just looking forward to meeting our new niece or nephew."

Maddie's lips stretched into a smile.

"Speaking of nieces and nephews…" Ali looked at Greer over Maddie's head. "Grant wants to know if there's anything we can do legally to ensure access to Layla. Are there visitation rights for uncles or something?"

Maddie made a sound. "Surely that's not necessary."

"It's been nearly six months," Ali said quietly. "Ryder hasn't made any attempts—"

"Has Grant?" Greer asked. She read the answer in Ali's expression. "Nothing will be accomplished if you and Grant take what Ryder will see as an adversarial angle."

Ali's chin came up. "And you know so much about Ryder's mind-set, do you?"

"I know that unless there's a custodial issue, a parent pretty much has the right to determine who has access to their own child!"

Ali looked annoyed.

"Remember that if it weren't for Ryder, Layla would have been adopted by now and off living in Florida where there would be *no* possibility at all for any of us to have some part in her life."

"That's right." Maddie was nodding. "Everyone just needs time. Things will work out for everyone. I know it will. We just have to have a little more patience. Meanwhile, I know there've been some problems with keeping a nanny, but Ray's last report to the court was positively glowing where Ryder's care of her is concerned."

"That's because Ryder *is* good with her. I've seen it for myself."

Both her sisters looked at her.

"I babysat for him last week. I filled in for Mrs. Pyle so she could be at court with her grandson."

Maddie's mouth formed an O. Ali looked annoyed.

"It was a last-minute decision," she added.

Ali held up her hand. "Thursday, Friday, Saturday." She ticked off on her fingers. "Sunday. Monday." She held up her hand. "Five days, Greer. It took you five days to tell us? What other secrets are you keeping?"

Greer pushed off the couch arm. "I'm not keeping secrets."

"What would you call it then?"

"Okay, fine." Ali had a point. "So I've…I've had a few encounters with Ryder lately."

Maddie's eyebrows rose. "A few?"

"How few?" Ali demanded. "And when?"

"Last week!" Greer hated feeling put on the hot seat, but knew she had only herself to blame for not telling them sooner. "I ran into him and Layla when I was on a break during court on Monday. It was just a coincidence." Though her chasing him right down the street hadn't been.

"So you think there's no reason to mention it?"

"No! I just—" She broke off. "I offered to help him find a nanny."

Maddie had closed her eyes and was breathing evenly. Ali, on the other hand, was watching Greer as though she'd committed a federal offense. "Why?"

"Because I wanted to help! You know that he was the one who got me to Maddie's shower."

"And why *did* he do that? He showed up just like that?" Ali snapped her fingers. "Out of the clear blue sky?"

"For God's sake, Ali. You're always suspicious. Yes, out of the clear blue sky! Maddie's been coaching us since you found Ryder not to push ourselves into his life until he gave some hint he'd welcome it. Well, he gave a hint! I didn't deliberately flag him down when I was stuck out by Devil's Crossing. But he helped and so I offered to help him in return. I'm not going to apologize for it. In fact, I would think you'd be glad for it!"

"Glad that you've been seeing my husband's *niece* without telling us a word about it? You *know* how important that is to Grant! Considering how estranged he'd been from Karen?"

Greer propped her fists on her hips. "I'm telling you now! Look, I know your husband is still dealing with his grief where his sister is concerned. But if he's been so concerned about Layla, why *hasn't he* gone banging on Ryder's door demanding to see her?" She waved at Maddie, who was looking pale. She'd always hated it when Greer and Ali went at it when they were kids, and things hadn't changed much since then. "Don't pretend that a man like your husband will follow *anyone's* advice if he doesn't agree with it! He blames Ryder and we all know it!"

"He *doesn't* blame Ryder! He blames himself!" Ali's raised voice echoed around the room. She was breathing hard. "And judging by Ryder's attitude these past months, he blames Grant, too."

The wind oozed out of Greer's sails. "Of course Grant's not responsible for what his sister did. Any more than Ryder is."

"I know that. And you know that. And my husband knows that, too. In here." Ali touched her forehead. "But in here," she said, tapping her chest, "it's still killing him."

Greer pushed aside the fruit and veggie tray and sat on the coffee table in front of her sisters. She grabbed Ali's hands and squeezed them. "It's not just hot monkey sex, right? The two of you are okay all the way around?"

Ali smiled slightly. She squeezed Greer's hands in return. "All the way around," she said huskily. "Grant is everything to me. I just want to be able to make this better for him."

"You will," Maddie murmured. "Just tell him about the baby."

"The baby," Greer echoed. "You think having another niece or nephew will make him less concerned with Layla?"

"Of course not," Maddie replied.

"She's talking about my baby."

Greer startled, looking at Ali. But Ali was looking at Maddie. "What I'd like to know is how *you* knew? I haven't told anyone yet that I'm pregnant!"

"I could just tell." Maddie blew out another audible breath as she scooted herself forward enough to push off the couch. "Now do me a favor, would you?" She pressed her hands against the small of her back and worked her way around the two of them. "Call *my* husband and tell him it's time."

Alarm slid through Greer's veins. "Time?"

"What d'you mean, *time*?" Ali looked even more alarmed.

"I mean baby time," Maddie exclaimed, thoroughly un-Maddie-like. "Now *move*!"

Chapter Six

The hands of the clock on the hospital waiting room wall seemed like they had stopped moving.

No matter how urgently Maddie had entered the hospital six hours earlier, time seemed to be crawling now.

Greer's dad was pacing the perimeter of the room, his steps measured and deliberate. Her mom, Meredith, was curled up in one of the chairs, her long hair spread over her updrawn knees. Vivian was sitting next to her, dozing lightly over the *Chronicle of Philanthropy* magazine on her lap. Archer was on his way from Denver, where he'd been consulting on a case, and Hayley and Seth had left only an hour ago, because it was long past time to put baby Keely to bed. Then there were Ali and Grant. Greer's brother-in-law wore the broody sort of expression that never really left his darkly handsome face. But there was still tenderness in his face as he looked down at Ali's tousled head on his shoulder. She was asleep.

"How much longer d'you think it will take?" Carter finally stopped in front of Meredith.

"I left my crystal ball at home." She looked amused. "It's a baby. It'll take as long as it takes."

Her dad made a face. "What if something's gone wrong?"

Meredith smiled gently and took his hand. "Nothing's gone wrong," she assured him.

"You don't know that. Things go wrong all the time."

"Carter." She stood, wrapping her arms around his waist and looking up at him. "It was only a few months ago that Hayley had Keely. That all went perfectly. And things are going to go perfectly with Maddie, too."

He pressed his cheek to the top of her head.

Frankly, Greer sympathized more with her dad. Things did go wrong all the time. Her career proved that on a daily basis.

What's happens to Layla if something happens to me?

"I'm going down to the cafeteria," she said, pushing away the thought. "Get myself a coffee. Can I bring back anything?"

Grant raised his hand. "Coffee here. I'll go, though."

Greer waved away his offer. "And wake Sleeping Beauty?" In the commotion of getting everyone to the hospital, Greer couldn't help but wonder if Ali had told him yet that they were expecting. She suspected not.

"Your dad'll take some coffee, too, sweetheart."

"I don't suppose there's a chance for a cocktail here?" Vivian commented, opening her eyes.

Carter grimaced. He didn't have a lot of affection for his mother, but since she'd moved to Wyoming in hopes of making amends with him after years of estrangement, he'd at least gotten to the point where it wasn't always open warfare with her whenever they were in the same room. "It's a hospital, Mother, not a bar."

"You never did have a sense of humor." Vivian looked at Greer with a twinkle in her eye as she patted her handbag sitting on the chair beside her. "I have my own flask with me for emergencies just like this. Just enough to make a cup of the dreadful coffee they have here a little more palatable."

Greer smiled, though it was anyone's guess whether or not Vivian was being serious. Not that it mattered to her if her grandmother wanted to spike her coffee while they waited for the baby to arrive. As far as she was concerned, nearly anything that got them through was fine. "I'll be back in a few."

She left the waiting room and started toward the elevator, but then aimed for the stairs instead to prolong her journey. As she passed the window of the nursery, she slowed to look inside. A dozen transparent bassinets were lined up, four of them holding tiny occupants, wrapped so snugly in white blankets that they looked more like burritos than miniature human beings.

A blonde nurse wearing rubber-ducky-patterned scrubs walked into view and picked up one of the baby burritos, affording Greer a brief view of a scrunched-up red face and a shock of dark hair before the nurse carried the baby out of sight again.

Greer lifted her hand and lightly touched the glass pane with her fingertips as she lingered there.

When Daisy had left Layla on Linc's doorstep, they'd estimated she was about two or three months old.

Looking at the babies inside the nursery, Greer still found it unfathomable how Daisy could have done such a thing. If she had lived, if she'd been charged with child endangerment, if her case had managed to land on Greer's desk like so many others, would she have been able to do her client justice?

The blonde nurse returned to the area with the bassinets. She didn't even glance toward the window, which made Greer wonder if the view was one-way. She plucked another baby from its bassinet, but instead of carrying the infant out of sight, she sat down in one of the rocking chairs situated around the nursery and cradled the baby to her shoulder as she began rocking.

Greer finally turned away, but the hollowness that had opened inside her wouldn't go away.

It was still there when she went down the cement-walled staircase, footsteps echoing loudly on the metal stairs. At the bottom, she pushed through the door, and realized that the staircase hadn't let her out in the lobby like the elevator would have, but in the emergency room.

Since there had been plenty of times when she'd had to visit a new client in Weaver's ER, she knew most of the shortcuts. She headed past the empty waiting area and the registration desk, aiming for the hallway on the other side that would take her back into the main part of the hospital.

"Hey, Greer. Heard that Maddie came in earlier. How's she doing?" the nurse behind the desk asked.

Greer slowed. "Six hours and still at it." She smiled at Courtney Hyde, who'd been an ER nurse since well before Greer had learned that they were cousins a few years ago. "Thought you didn't work nights anymore?"

Courtney tucked her long gold hair behind her ear. "Don't usually. But we're shorthanded at the moment, so." She shrugged. "We're all doing our part." Then she smiled a little impishly. "And it gives Sadie an opportunity to have her daddy all to herself at bedtime. Yesterday when I got home, she'd convinced Mason

to build her an 'ice palace'—" she air-quoted the term
"—to sleep in, using every pillow and furniture cushion we have in the house. Sadie slept the divine sleep
that only a three-year-old can sleep."

"And Mason?"

Courtney grinned. "My big tough husband had me
schedule him for a massage just so he could work out
the kinks from a night spent on the floor crammed inside an igloo of pillows."

Considering the fact that Mason Hyde was about six
and a half feet tall, Greer could well believe it.

"I swear I'll never stop melting inside whenever I see
the way he is with her, though," Courtney added, sighing a little. "Just wait. Someday you'll see what I mean."

Greer kept her smile in place, even though the image
inside her head wasn't one of Mason Hyde and his little
girl. It was of Ryder, scooping Cow Pie Surprise into
Layla's greedy mouth.

"You going to be at the picnic?"

"Sorry?"

"Gloria and Squire are hosting a big ol' picnic next
week out at the Double C. To celebrate Labor Day.
Whole family will be there." Courtney's eyes twin-
kled. "That includes all of you Templetons now, too."

Greer chuckled wryly. "I kind of need to show my
face at the county employee picnic that weekend. My
boss's wife organizes it. Besides which, just because
the Clay family lines have expanded our way doesn't
necessarily mean we're welcome. If *my* grandmother
finds out we're consorting with *your* grandfather, who
knows how bad the fireworks will be."

"Old wounds," Courtney said dismissively. "Vivian
might have shunned Squire's first wife sixty years ago,
but she's apologized. It's high time he let it go. At least

think about the picnic." She reached out an arm and picked up the phone when it started ringing. "Emergency," she answered. "Think about it," she mouthed silently to Greer.

Nodding, Greer left the other woman to her duties and continued on her way, only to stop short again when the double doors leading to the exam rooms swung open and Ryder appeared. He was holding Layla, wrapped in a blanket.

Alarm exploded inside her.

When he spotted her, his dark brows pulled together over his bloodshot blue eyes. He stopped several feet away. "What're you doing here?"

"What are *you* doing here?" Without thought, she closed the distance between them and put her hand on Layla's back through the blanket. The toddler's head was resting on his shoulder. Her eyes were closed, her cheeks flushed. "What's wrong?"

"Nothing."

The comment came from Caleb Buchanan, and Greer realized the pediatrician had followed Ryder through the double doors. "However, if she hasn't improved in the next twenty-four hours, give me or her regular pediatrician a call."

"Thanks." Ryder's jaw was dark with stubble and he looked like he hadn't slept in a couple days.

"And don't worry too much," Caleb added. "Kids run fevers. As long as it doesn't get too high, her body's just doing what it's supposed to do."

When Ryder nodded, Caleb transferred his focus to Greer. "Heard Maddie was here. How's everyone doing?" Thanks to the prolificacy of Squire Clay's side of the family, Caleb was also a cousin. His pale blue scrubs did nothing to disguise his Superman-like physique. But Greer knew from experience that the doctor was singularly unconcerned with his looks.

"Fine. Anxious for the baby to get here. We've been waiting hours."

"Want me to check in on them?"

"That'd be great, if you've got the time. Everyone's up in the waiting room. I was just gonna grab some coffees from the cafeteria."

He smiled and patted her shoulder. "I'll see what I can find out." Then he retreated through the double doors.

Greer immediately focused on Ryder again. "How long has she been sick?"

"She didn't eat much of her dinner, but she seemed okay until she woke up crying a couple hours ago." He shifted the baby to his other shoulder. Layla didn't stir. "She threw up all over her crib, then threw up all over me and was hot as a pistol."

Greer couldn't help herself. She rubbed her hand soothingly over the thin blanket and the warm little body beneath. "Poor baby."

"Speaking of. Your sister's having hers?"

She nodded. "Whole family's been here at some point tonight."

"Hope everything goes okay." He took a step toward the sliding glass entrance doors.

"Ryder—"

He hesitated, waiting.

She wasn't sure why her mouth felt dry all of a sudden, but it did. "I...I haven't heard anything on the job postings yet. Have you?"

He shook his head. "Mrs. Pyle said she'd give me the rest of this week, after all." He shifted from one cowboy boot to the other. "Think she's feeling in a good mood after her grandson's acquittal last week."

"But not good enough to stay on indefinitely."

"She's a housekeeper. Not—"

"—a nanny," Greer finished along with him. "Well, I should get back up to the waiting room. They're probably wondering what's keeping me." She chewed the inside of her cheek. "I don't suppose you want to come…"

He was shaking his head even before her words trailed off. "Need to get her back in her own bed." He grimaced a little. "After I've gotten it all restored to rights, at least."

"Of course." She pushed her hands down into the back pockets of her lightweight cotton pants. It was silly of her to even have the notion. "Well." She edged toward the elevator. "Fingers crossed someone nibbles at one of the job posts."

The corner of his mouth lifted slightly and she felt certain he was thinking more about his wife idea than the nanny. "Yeah."

She took two more steps toward the elevator and jabbed her finger against the call button.

"Don't forget the cafeteria."

"What?" Her face warmed. "Oh. Right." The elevator doors slid open but she ignored them.

He smiled faintly. "G'night, Counselor."

She managed a faint smile, too, though it felt unsteady. "Good night, Ryder."

He carried Layla through the sliding door and disappeared into the darkness.

Greer swallowed and moistened her lips, then nearly jumped out of her skin when Courtney walked up and stopped next to her. She was carrying a stack of medical charts. "If I weren't already head over heels for my husband," she whispered conspiratorially, "I'd probably be sighing a little myself over that one."

"I'm not *sighing* over him."

Courtney grinned. "Sure you're not." With a quick wink, she backed her way through the double doors.

Left alone in the tiled room, Greer pressed her palms against her warm cheeks. She shook her head, trying to shake it off.

But it was no use.

And then her cell phone buzzed with a text from Ali. Where are u?! Baby here!

Forget the coffee.

She pushed the phone back into her pocket and darted for the elevator.

"If we're keeping you awake, Ms. Templeton, maybe you should consider another line of work."

Greer stared guiltily up at Judge Manetti as she tried to stop her yawn. It was a futile effort, though.

Just because she'd been at the hospital until three this morning celebrating the birth of her new nephew didn't mean she'd been allowed a respite from her duties at work.

"I'm sorry, Your Honor," she said once she could speak clearly. In the year since Steve Manetti had gone from being a fellow attorney to being a municipal court judge appointed by the mayor, she had almost gotten used to addressing him as such. But it had been hard, considering they'd been in elementary school together.

She glanced down at her copy of the day's docket before slipping the correct case file to the top of her pile. "My client, Mr. Jameson, wishes to enter a plea of not guilty."

Manetti looked resigned. "Of course he does." He

looked over his steepled fingers at the skinny man standing hunched beside her. "Is that correct, Mr. Jameson?"

Johnny Jameson nodded jerkily. Every motion since he'd entered the courtroom betrayed the fact that he was high on something. Undoubtedly meth, which was what he was charged with possessing. Again. "Yessir."

Manetti looked at Greer, then down at his court calendar. "First available looks like the second Thursday of December."

She made a note. "Thank you, Your Honor."

Judge Manetti looked at the clock on the wall, then at the bailiff. "We'll break for lunch now."

"All rise," the bailiff intoned, and the small municipal courtroom filled with the rustling sounds of people standing. Manetti disappeared through his door and the courtroom started emptying.

Greer closed her case file and fixed her gaze on her client. "Johnny, the judge just gave you four months. I advise you to clean up your act before trial. Understand me?"

Johnny shrugged and twitched and avoided meeting her eyes. She shifted focus to Johnny's wife behind him. "Katie? Do you want another copy of the list of programs I gave you before?"

"No, ma'am." Katie Jameson was petite and polite and as clean as her husband was not. "Johnny's gonna be just fine by then. I promise you."

Greer dearly wished she could believe it. "All right, then." She pushed her files into her briefcase and shouldered the strap. "You know how to reach me if you need me. Mr. Chatham will be in touch with you to go through your testimony before December."

Johnny grunted a reply and shuffled his way out of the courtroom.

"You're a lot nicer than Mr. Chatham," Katie said, watching her husband go. "I wish you could handle Johnny's trial."

Greer smiled. "Don't worry. You and Johnny will be in good hands."

"Well, thank you for everything you've done so far."

It was a rare day when Greer received thanks for her service. More often than not, she busted her butt negotiating a deal for her client only to have him or her walk away without a single word of appreciation. She shook Katie's hand. "You're welcome, Katie. Take care of yourself, okay? I meant it when I said you can call if you need me."

The young woman nodded, ducking her chin a little, then hurried after her husband.

Greer stifled another yawn as she walked out of the courtroom. She had two hours before her next appearance. If she'd had more than a few dollars left in her bank account after spending most of her paycheck on bills, she would have gone down to Josephine's for a sandwich. Instead, she walked back to her office, where she closed the door and kicked off her pumps. Then she sat down at her desk, and with a good old peanut-butter-and-jelly sandwich in one hand and a pencil in the other, she started in on the messages she hadn't been able to respond to before morning court.

She'd been at it for barely an hour when her office door opened and her boss tossed another stack of papers on her desk. "We're not getting an intern this round. There were only two available and the other offices needed them more." He pointed at the papers he'd left. "Plead all those out."

She swallowed the bite of sandwich that had momentarily stuck to the roof of her mouth and thumbed the latest pile. "What if they don't all want to plead?" She knew the futility of the question, but asked out of habit.

"Talk them into it," he said, and then left as unceremoniously as he'd entered. He always said that. Even though he knew some cases and some defendants never would plead.

Or should.

She glanced at the clock above the door. She started to lift her sandwich to her mouth, but her phone rang and she answered it. "Public defender's office."

There was a faint hesitation before a female spoke. "I'm calling about the job posting? The one for a nanny?"

Greer sat up straighter.

"This is the right number, isn't it?" The woman had a faint accent that Greer couldn't place. "You said public defender's office?"

"Yes, yes, it's the right number." She set her sandwich down on the plastic wrap. "I'm Greer Templeton. I represent—" She cringed, realizing how that might sound. "I'm *assisting* a friend with his search for a nanny."

"He's not in trouble with the law?"

"No, not at all."

"That's a relief," the woman said with a little laugh. "The last thing I desire is another job that leaves me wanting. I prefer something that will be steady. And lasting. Your post said you're—he, your friend—is looking for a live-in? Is that written in stone?"

"It's probably negotiable. Why don't you give me your contact information and you can discuss it with him directly."

"Very good. My name is Eliane Dupre."

"Would you mind spelling—"

The caller laughed lightly. "Like Elaine but reverse the *i* and *a*. It's French."

Greer immediately imagined a beautiful, chic Parisian singing French lullabies to Layla while Ryder looked on. She cleared her throat, and her head of the image. "Is that where you're from? France?"

"Switzerland, actually. I moved to the States a few years ago with my husband. Alas, that didn't work out, but here I am. I'm a citizen," she said quickly, "in case that is a concern."

Her right to work should have been more of a concern to Greer, but her imagination was still going bananas. Swiss? Had Maria in *The Sound of Music* been Swiss? She sure got her man. No, that was Austria.

Still, the loving governess had captured the heart of the children and their father.

She shook her head at her own nonsense, making notes as Eliane provided her phone number and an address in Weaver in her musical, accented voice.

"You understand that the location where you'd be working is fairly remote?"

"Yes. Quite to my liking."

"How long have you lived in Weaver?"

"I've only been here a few weeks. I'm staying with an acquaintance while I look for employment. Shall I expect a call from your friend, then?"

There was no reason to hesitate, but Greer still felt like she had to push her way through the conversation. "Yes, I'll get your information to him as soon as I can."

"Thank you so much. Have a lovely day."

"You, too," Greer said faintly. But she said it to the dial tone, because Eliane had already ended the call.

She dropped the receiver back on the cradle and stared blindly at her notes. Then she snatched up the phone again and punched out Ryder's phone number.

Neither Mrs. Pyle, Ryder nor the machine picked up.

Was Layla still sick? Maybe Ryder had caught whatever bug she'd had. Or maybe her fever had gotten worse.

Greer rubbed at the pain between her eyebrows. "Stop imagining things," she muttered, "and be logical here."

She pulled up the information she had on record for Anthony Pyle. But when she called that number, there was no answer.

She hung up and looked at the time. She couldn't very well drive Eliane's information out to the Diamond-L and check on Ryder and Layla herself. Not when she was supposed to be back in court in less than an hour.

She looked at the docket she'd printed that morning. Hearing conferences and motions.

She reached for the phone again and dialed. This time, she received an answer. "Keith? It's Greer. Can you pinch-hit for me this afternoon? I know it's short notice, but I have a personal matter that's come up."

"Personal matter!" He sounded surprised. "You're joking, right?"

She made a face at the wall. "Does it sound like I'm joking?"

He chuckled. "I'm just yanking your chain. Nice to know that you're human like the rest of us. So, yeah. Sure. Just for today?"

"Just for today. I'll leave my files at the front desk with Bunny. Court's back in session at two."

"I'll be there," he promised. "Everything all right? I heard Maddie had the baby last night—"

"They're all fine," she assured him. It never failed to

surprise her how quickly news spread in this town. "It's nothing to do with that. I really appreciate the favor. I'll owe you one."

"And I plan on collecting," he said with a laugh before hanging up.

Now that she'd made the decision, she tossed the rest of her sandwich in the trash. The bread was already getting stale, anyway. She bundled up everything that Keith might need for the afternoon and left it with Bunny Towers. Then she went back to retrieve her shoes and purse and left the office.

Not even Michael noticed, which had her wondering why she'd never tried taking off an afternoon before. No matter what she did, her boss seemed to remain unimpressed.

It took nearly an hour to get to Ryder's place. There were no vehicles parked on the gravel outside the house. Even though she'd seen it more than once now, the sight of the converted barn was still arresting. The only barn conversions she'd ever seen before were in magazines and on home decorating shows.

No doubt, Eliane-of-the-beautiful-accent would only add another layer of interest to the surroundings.

"Get your brain out of high school," she muttered, and snatched up her purse before marching to the front door. There was no answer when she knocked, but the door was unlocked when she tried it. She cautiously pushed it open. "Hello? Mrs. Pyle?" She stepped inside. "Ryder?"

The last time she'd been there, the house had been as tidy as a pin.

Now it looked like a tornado had hit.

Layla's toys were everywhere. Laundry was piled on the armless chair, overflowing onto the floor. The couch was nearly hidden beneath a plastic bin that she felt certain contained the baby gear that Maddie and Linc had given Ryder when they'd turned Layla over to him.

She dropped her purse on top of it and walked into the kitchen. Cereal crunched under her shoes. The sink was filled halfway to the top with dirty dishes.

She crunched her way to the back door and looked out at the picnic table with its painted daisies. It hadn't even been a week since she'd been there, but the grass was already overgrown.

Weren't Swiss people notoriously tidy? Maybe Eliane would take one look and run for the hills.

The thought should have been worrying.

The fact that it was not was an entirely different cause for concern.

She left the door open slightly to allow for some fresh air—hot as it was—and went upstairs.

Layla's nursery was empty. The mattress had been stripped of bedding. It was probably sitting in the pile of laundry downstairs.

The air was stuffy here, too. One window held a boxy air conditioner. It wasn't running, and Greer left it off. She went to the second window and opened it; the hot breeze fluttered at the simple white curtains.

She left Layla's room, intending to go back downstairs, but she hesitated, looking down the hall toward the other open door. She could see the foot of a bed where a navy blue quilt was piled half on and half off the mattress. A pair of cowboy boots were lying haphazardly on the wood floor.

Unquestionably, the room was Ryder's.

When she'd babysat Layla, the sliding door to the room had been closed.

She knew the house was empty.

Still, Greer's heart beat a little faster as she stepped closer to the room. She peered around the edge of the doorway. The dresser was wide, with six drawers. One framed picture sat on top, but otherwise it was bare.

His bed was big with an iron-railed headboard. Three white pillows were bunched messily at the head of the mattress. Instead of a nightstand next to the bed, there was a saddletree complete with a fancy-looking tooled leather saddle. An industrial sort of lamp was attached directly to the wall. There was an enormous unadorned window next to the bed, and before she knew it, she'd walked across the room to look out.

Directly below was the picnic table.

She wondered how often he looked out and thought about his late wife.

She wondered if he'd look out and still think about her when he had a delectable Swiss confection under his roof tending to his child.

Disgusted with herself, she turned away from the window. She bent down slightly to look at the framed photograph on his dresser. It was an old-fashioned black-and-white wedding photo. Maybe his parents? Or the aunt named Adelaide? Then she heard a faint sound and her nervousness ratcheted up.

She darted out of the bedroom and was heading to the staircase when Ryder—looking entirely incongruous in cowboy hat and boots with a pink-patterned baby carrier strapped across his chest—appeared.

Even before he saw her, his eyes were narrowed. "What're you doing here?"

Chapter Seven

What're you doing here?

Ryder's question seemed to echo around her.

He looked hot and sweaty, as did Layla in the carrier, and Greer's mouth went dry.

Not only from nearly being caught out snooping in his bedroom, but from the strange swooping feeling in her stomach caused by the sight of him.

"Greer?"

She felt like her brains were scrambled and gestured vaguely toward Layla's bedroom. "I was...ah—"

"Never mind." In a move that she knew from personal experience was more difficult than he made it look, he unfastened Layla from the carrier and handed her to Greer. "Take her for a few minutes while I clean up."

Layla's green eyes were bright and merry as she looked at Greer. She was wearing a yellow T-shirt that felt damp and a pair of yellow shorts with a ruffle across her butt. Her reddish-blond curls were spiked with perspiration. "Is she still running a fever?"

"Nah. Even on a cold day the carrier gets hot." He pulled off his hat as he brushed past Greer, smelling like sunshine and fresh hay. He continued along the hallway, pulling off not only the carrier, but his T-shirt, as well. "She popped out two more teeth this morning, though. I don't care what that doc said last night about teething not causing a fever. Soon as those teeth showed up, she was right as rain, just like my aunt Adelaide predicted." He stepped inside his bedroom and looked at Greer. "Be down in a few." Then he pulled on the rustic metal handle and slid the door closed.

She closed her eyes. But the image of his bare chest remained.

Heaven help her.

She opened them again to find Layla smiling brightly at her, displaying the new additions to her bottom row of teeth. She jabbered and patted Greer's face.

Greer caught the baby's hand and kissed it. "Hello to you, too, sweetheart."

She heard a couple thuds from behind Ryder's bedroom door. It was much too easy imagining him sitting on the foot of that messy, wide bed, pulling off his boots and tossing them aside.

After the boots would come the jeans—

"Let's go downstairs," she whispered quickly to Layla, who laughed as if Greer had said something wonderfully funny.

"At least *you* think it's funny." Greer hurried to the staircase. "You have a lot in common with your aunt Ali, that's for sure."

Once downstairs, she settled Layla into her high

chair. It was much cleaner than the kitchen counters were, so she had to give Ryder points for that.

She opened the back door wider so there was more air flowing, then found a clean cloth in a drawer. She wet it down with cool water and worked it over Layla's face and head. Layla took it as a game, of course, and slyly evaded most of Greer's swipes before gaining control of the cloth, which she proceeded to shove into her mouth.

Chewing on a wet washcloth wasn't the worst thing Greer could think of, so she let the baby have it and turned her attention to the dishes in the sink. They weren't quite as dirty as she'd first thought. At least they'd been rinsed.

Loading the dishwasher didn't take much time. She found the soap and started it. But the sound of the dishwasher wasn't enough to block the sound of water running overhead, and Greer's imagination ran amok again.

To combat it, she found another cloth and furiously began wiping down the counters. When she was done with that, she found the broom and swept up the scattered cereal crumbs. And when she was done with *that*, she grabbed an armful of clothes from the pile on the chair and blindly shoved it into the washing machine located in a sunny room right off the kitchen.

The cheeriness of the room was almost enough to make up for the laundry drudgery, and she wondered if he'd made it that way for Daisy.

With the washing machine now running, too, she went back into the kitchen, lifted Layla out of the high chair and took her outside.

"You like this soft grass as much as I do?" Greer unfastened the narrow straps around her ankles and kicked off her high-heeled shoes, curling her toes in the tall grass. She bent over Layla, holding her hands as the baby pushed up and down on her bent knees, chortling.

"Wait until next year. You're going to be running all over the grass on your own." They slowly aimed toward the picnic table. But they made it only partway before Layla plopped down on her diaper-padded, ruffle-covered butt. She grabbed at the grass undulating around her and yanked, then looked surprised when the soft blades tore free.

Greer tugged her skirt above her knees so she could sit in the grass with her. She mimicked Layla's grass grab and then held open her hands so the pieces of green blew away on the breeze.

Layla opened her palms and her grass blew away, too. Instead of laughing, though, her brows pulled together and her face scrunched.

Greer laughed. "Silly girl." She tore off another handful of grass and let it go again. "See it blow away?" She leaned over and nuzzled her nose against Layla's palms. "Smells so good." Then she rubbed her nose against Layla's and plucked a single blade of grass and tickled her cheek with the end of it. "Smells kind of like your daddy, doesn't it?"

"Mama mamamama!" Layla laughed and grabbed the grass, but missed and rolled onto her side. She immediately popped up and crawled over to Greer, clambering onto her lap.

Knowing Layla hadn't really said *mama* didn't stop Greer's heart from lurching. She wrapped her arm around Layla's warm body and kissed the top of her head.

Then they both yanked hunks of grass free and tossed them into the air.

He had a perfect view of them from his bedroom window.

Ryder dragged the towel over his head and down his

chest. The water in the shower hadn't been much above tepid to begin with, but it had turned altogether cold after only a few minutes.

Probably a good thing.

Below, Layla had crawled onto Greer's lap. As he watched, Greer rolled onto her back, heedless of her silk blouse and her hair that today had been pulled back into a smooth knot behind her head. She pushed Layla up into the air above her, and even through his closed window, he could hear her peals of laughter.

He'd been cursing Mrs. Pyle's absence after she'd promised him another week of work. With no alternative, it had meant hauling a baby around with him on a tractor for half the day. Which meant he still wasn't finished haying. He was falling behind on everything.

But right now, looking down at Greer and the baby, he almost didn't care.

Almost.

As if she sensed him watching, Greer suddenly looked up at his window. It was too far for him to see her exact expression, but he had no trouble imagining her dark brown eyes.

They were mesmerizing, those eyes of hers. They kept entering his thoughts at all hours of the day.

And the night.

The air-conditioner kicked on, blowing cold air over him and drowning out the sound of Layla's high-pitched squeals.

He took a step back and blew out a long breath, not even aware that he'd been holding it.

"You're losing it, man," he muttered to himself, roughly dragging the towel over his head once more before tossing it aside. It knocked over his grandparents' picture and he automatically set it to rights while he pulled out the last clean shirt he possessed, plus a pair of jeans that weren't so clean. He quickly got dressed and went downstairs.

As soon as he walked through the kitchen, he understood why his shower water had been cold. Both the washing machine and the dishwasher were going.

It wasn't Mrs. Pyle's doing, that was for certain.

The mug tree sitting on one corner of the butcher-block island had three clean mugs still hanging from the metal branches. He took two, filled them with water and pushed open the wooden screen door.

When it slammed shut behind him, Greer froze and looked his way. Her face was as flushed as Layla's and dark strands of hair had worked loose to cling to her neck.

The ivory blouse she wore had come partially free from the waist of her light gray skirt. As if she were following the progression of his gaze, she suddenly pushed the hem of her skirt down her thighs and swept her legs to one side as she set Layla down on the grass. "It's still crazy hot," she commented, not exactly looking his way. "What happened to Mrs. Pyle?"

"Her grandson." He was as barefoot as the two females, and the earth beneath his feet felt cooler than anything else as he walked toward them. It was no wonder Greer had chosen to sit in the grass rather than at the picnic table. He extended one of the mugs to her. "It's just water."

She smiled a little as she took it from him. "Thank you." Before she could get the cup to her mouth, though, Layla launched herself at it, and Greer wasn't quite quick enough to avoid her. Half the water sloshed out of the cup and onto her blouse, rendering several inches of silky fabric nearly transparent.

Ryder was polite enough not to comment, but too male to look away. He could see the scrolling lacework of blue thread beneath the wet patch and had no trouble at all imagining the soft flesh beneath that.

Greer plucked at the fabric, though as far as he could tell, she only succeeded in pulling the rest of the blouse loose from the skirt. She took a sip of what was left of the water, then held it to Layla's mouth. "What's going on with Anthony? He was just acquitted last week."

"And he turned around and got picked up on drunk driving last night."

She jerked, giving him a sharp look that was echoed somewhat by the sharp look that Layla gave *her*. "What? Where? I haven't heard about it."

"I don't know where." He sat on the grass, leaning his back against the picnic table. "I just know she dropped everything and immediately took off to rescue him." Mrs. Pyle had given him the courtesy of a rushed phone call, but that was it.

Greer frowned, then focused once more on Layla, who'd started fussing for the mug of water. "I'm sorry, sweetheart. It's empty now. See?" She turned the mug upside down and glanced back at Ryder. "You make that sound like a bad thing."

"I don't have a lot of sympathy for people who drink and drive."

"Because of what happened to Layla's mother."

"Because of what happened to my mother." The second the words were out, he regretted them. "Here." He leaned forward and poured half his water into her mug, then sat back again. "You obviously didn't come out here because Mrs. Pyle asked you to sub for her." He repeated what he'd asked when he walked into his house and found her there. "So what *are* you doing here?"

"Someone called me about the nanny position."

"You must be pretty excited about the prospect to drive out here to tell me. I do have a phone, you know."

"Which nobody answered when I called. And then after last night… Layla's fever and all." She lifted one shoulder, watching Layla, who'd lost interest in the mug and had started crawling toward the far side of the picnic table. "I was concerned. So I drove out."

"And found the place looking like a bomb had hit."

"You want me to say it wasn't that bad?"

"I have a feeling you're not much for lies, even the polite ones."

She got on her hands and knees and crawled after Layla. "I did watch her for the better part of a day," she reminded him. "I can appreciate that she's kind of a force of nature." She looked over her shoulder at him for a moment. "Toss in last night's trip to the hospital, and a messy house doesn't seem so strange."

The afternoon was admittedly hot. But that wasn't the cause for the furnace suddenly cranking up inside him. He looked away from the shapely butt closely outlined by pale gray fabric. "What did she sound like?"

"Who? Oh, right." Greer pushed herself up to sit on the bench. "Her name's Eliane. Eliane Dupre."

"French."

She gave him a surprised look.

"I knew an Eliane once."

Surprise slid into something else. Something on the verge of pinched and suspicious. "Oh?"

"She was a model for Adelaide during her nudes phase."

"Excuse me?"

"My aunt's an artist." And Eliane had been an incredible tutor for a horny seventeen-year-old. He didn't share that part, though, much as he was coming to enjoy the game of keeping the lady lawyer a little off-balance. It was his one way of feeling like things were sort of even between them. "What else did you learn besides her name?"

Greer was still giving him a measuring look.

Or maybe she was just trying to keep her eye from twitching.

"She's currently staying in Weaver. She did ask if the live-in part was negotiable. So when you talk with her, be prepared."

"What else?"

"She's from Switzerland. Divorced, it sounds like. And looking for a steady job. I have her phone number in my purse."

He pushed to his feet. "Let's do it, then."

Greer's expression didn't change as she lifted Layla and stood. But he still had the sense that he'd surprised her. And not necessarily in a good way.

They went inside and she handed him a slip of paper from her purse. Then she carried Layla back outside.

To give him privacy? Or because she wasn't interested in the conversation in the first place?

Even wondering was stupid. Pointless.

Maybe he needed more sleep.

He snatched the phone off the hook and looked at the paper.

Greer's handwriting was slightly slanted and neat. *Spare*, as Adelaide would say. There were no curlicues. No extra tails or circles. While he dialed the number, his mind's eye imagined her hand quickly recording the information on the paper.

Daisy's handwriting had been all over the place. All loopy letters and heart-dotted *i*'s.

He pushed away the thought. He definitely needed more sleep.

The phone rang four times before it went to voice mail. He wasn't sure if he was disappointed or not. He left his name and number and hung up, then went back outside. It was hotter outside than in, but at least the air was moving.

This time Greer was sitting at the table bouncing Layla on her lap.

"No answer. I left a message."

"I'm sure she'll call you back. She sounded pretty interested to me."

The wet patch on her blouse had dried. No more intriguing glimpses of white lace with blue threads. But there was a smudge of green on her thigh. "You have grass stains."

Her eyebrows rose, then she quickly looked down at herself. She swiped her hand at the mark. "Dry cleaners will get it out. Hopefully." Her shoulders rose and fell as she took a deep breath. "I should be going."

"Back to the office, I suppose."

She glanced at the narrow watch on her wrist. "Court should be finished for the day, but yes, I probably should go back. Start reviewing everything for tomorrow's docket."

"Probably." He waited a beat, but she didn't move an inch. "Or—"

Her gaze slid toward him.

"Or I could pull out a couple steaks." He jerked his thumb toward the covered grill. "Throw 'em on the grill after I give Short-Stuff a badly needed bath."

Greer's lips parted slightly. The top one was a little fuller than the bottom, he realized.

"Or you could give her a bath," he said casually. "If you wanted."

Her lips twitched. "I do like steak. Medium rare."

"I wouldn't do well-done even if you asked."

She ran her fingers over Layla's curls. "You feed her *after* her bath?"

"Counselor, sometimes I'm feeding her ten times a day. I learned real quick there's no point in sweating about the order of things when it comes to her."

"My mother would love you," she murmured. She stood with Layla. "And I'm clearly not above a bribe, whether there's dinner payment or not." She marched past him into the house.

He scrubbed his hand down his face and followed her inside. She was fastening Layla into the high chair.

"Have any of your cow pie stuff?"

"Not today." He took the last banana from the holder and started peeling it. "Personally, I hate bananas, but she loves 'em." He tossed the browning peel in the trash, then cut the fruit into small chunks and dropped them into a shallow plastic bowl that he set in front of Layla.

She was already starting to look heavy-lidded, but she dived into the bowl with both hands. "Greedy girl." He plucked a mushy piece of banana from her cheek and fed it to her.

Greer was watching him when he turned away. "What?"

She just shook her head slightly and cleared her throat. "What else besides overripe banana? Does she still have a bottle?"

"Formula, but she wants it in her cup." He looked in the sink.

"I loaded everything in the dishwasher."

He pulled it open and steam spewed out. He plucked

out the cup and lid, then closed the door and started it up again. He rinsed both pieces under cold water, then filled it with premixed formula. "There's a container in the fridge with some cooked vegetables. She didn't eat 'em last night."

Greer went to the refrigerator and opened it.

He glanced over. "Top shelf. Red lid."

She pulled out the glass container and peeled off the lid. "Yum. Carrots and peas."

"Don't knock it." He gave Layla her sippy cup, then took the container from Greer, dumped the vegetables in a pan and set it on the stove.

"Wouldn't the microwave be faster?"

"Yep." He made a face as he lit the flame under the pan. "Adelaide'll lecture me for a week about the dangers."

"There are dangers?"

"Probably not as many as my aunt can name." He jabbed a spoon at the vegetables. "It's one of those lose-the-battle-win-the-war things, I think."

"You're in a war with the microwave?"

He chuckled. "More like a war with my aunt over the microwave. You might say she's a little—" He broke off when the phone rang. "Eccentric," he finished. "Watch these, would you?"

"An eccentric aunt who paints nudes and names her dog Brutus. She sounds like quite a woman. You mention her a lot." Greer's fingers brushed his as she took over the spoon. "Afraid I'm not much of a cook."

"She photographs nudes," he corrected. "Among other things. And I'm afraid I'm not much of a cook, either. But I like to eat, so—" He picked up the ringing phone. "Diamond-L."

"Is this Mr. Wilson?" The voice was female. Accented. "I'm Eliane Dupre."

"Eliane," he repeated, watching Greer turn toward the stove so that her slender back was to him.

Her shoulders were noticeably tight beneath the thin, silky blouse.

Interesting.

The conversation was brief.

Greer's back was still to him when he hung up. She was stirring the vegetables so diligently, he figured they'd end up mushier than the banana. He moved next to her and turned off the heat beneath the pan.

"I'm meeting her tomorrow over lunch at Josephine's," he said.

She gave him an overbright smile. "Great." She brushed her hands down the sides of her skirt. "You know, I just remembered I *do* have to go back to the office before tomorrow morning. So I'm going to have to pass on the bribery, after all." As she spoke, she was backing out of the kitchen, stopping only long enough to lean over and kiss Layla's head as she passed.

"You sure?" He tested the vegetables. Definitely mushy. But at least not too hot. He dumped some into Layla's now-empty banana bowl.

Greer's head bobbed. "I'm sure. Let me know how it, uh, how it goes tomorrow." She grabbed her purse that was sitting on the couch and clutched it to her waist with both hands.

"Will do."

"Great." Her head bobbed a few more times. "Well, good…good luck." She quickly turned on her bare feet and hurried to the front door.

"By the way, what did she have?"

She'd made it to the vestibule and she gave him a startled look. "Excuse me?"

"Your sister."

She looked even more deer-in-the-headlights. "Maddie! She had a boy. Seven pounds, thirteen ounces. Twenty-one inches long. They named him Liam Gustav after Linc's grandfather. Mommy and son are doing well." She smiled quickly and yanked open the front door. "Daddy is, reportedly, a basket case." She lifted her hand in a quick wave and darted out the door, closing it behind her.

He waited.

But she didn't come back.

Even though her feet were bare, since her high-heeled pumps were still out back, lying in the grass.

He looked at Layla.

She was plucking a pea out of the carrots with one hand and clutching her pink cup with the other.

"Interesting, indeed," he told her.

She smacked her cup against the high chair tray and gave him a beatific smile. "Bye bye bye bye!"

"You got that right, Short-Stuff. She sure did go bye-bye." He chucked her lightly under the chin. "But I'm betting she'll be back."

Chapter Eight

"What the hell did you do to your feet?"

Greer looked up to see Ali standing in the doorway to her office and yanked her feet down from where they were propped on the corner of her desk. "Nothing." She tugged her black skirt down around her knees.

"You have bandage strips all over the soles of your feet."

"I know you're in uniform, but you can stop the interrogation. Bandage strips aren't a criminal offense." Greer slid her feet into the shoes under her desk. She was still embarrassed over the way she'd raced out of Ryder's place the evening before. She didn't particularly want to explain why to her sister. "What brings you to the dark side?"

"Glad you're finally ready to admit the truth about your work." Ali grinned and threw herself down on the chair inside the doorway. She leaned back and propped her heavy department-issue boots on the corner of the desk.

"Hey!" Greer shoved at them. "Just because I did, doesn't mean you can. Have a little respect, please."

"For the dark side? Never." She put her feet on the floor, still smiling.

"You're in an awfully good mood," Greer complained. "If you've come to brag about the latest night or morning or afternoon of hot sex you've had with your new husband, spare me."

Ali looked at her fingernails. "Well, it is pretty bragworthy," she drawled.

"Save me."

"You don't need saving. You need sexing."

"Ali, for God's sake."

Her sister laughed silently. "Your chain is so easy to yank these days."

"And if you weren't pregnant, I'd yank yours but good. Speaking of." She pinned her sister with her fiercest lawyer look. "Have you told Grant?"

"Yes."

"And?"

"Between looking like he wanted to pass out and suddenly treating me like I'm made of Dresden Porcelain, I think he's pretty much okay with it." Her expression sobered. "He still needs to create some kind of relationship with Layla, though. He's not going to let it go, Greer. He can't."

"Nor should he even think he has to." She dropped her head onto her hands, pressing her fingertips into her scalp. She exhaled and lifted her head. "Ryder's coming along, Ali." She hoped. "Is that what you came here to find out?"

"Actually, I came here to invite you to lunch. Josephine's. On me."

"Oh, that's right. You're not living only on a public

servant's salary anymore. You have a bestselling thriller writer as a husband now."

"Poke as much as you want. Do you care for a free lunch or don't you?"

"I do." She glanced at her watch. "It'll have to be quick, though. I have less than an hour before I need to be over at the courthouse."

"Yeah, yeah." Ali pushed to her feet. "I know the drill. Josephine's pretty much makes a living off the police department and the courthouse. It's always quick." She waited while Greer collected her purse and they left her office. "Seriously." Ali gave her a sidelong look. "What is going on with your feet? You're limping. You didn't actually fall through one of the floorboards in the kitchen, did you?"

"Of course not. I just, uh, just broke a glass."

Ali pushed through the entrance door first. "You never could lie for squat." She stopped short. "Hello, Mr. Towers. Out enjoying the weather?" She smiled the same sweet smile she'd used all her life when she didn't particularly like someone. "I've heard you like things hot."

Michael looked right through Ali to focus on Greer. "I learned that you didn't take the plea on Dilley."

"The client refused."

Her boss looked particularly annoyed. "I told you to plead them all."

"I cannot force a client to accept a deal! Particularly one that isn't even a good deal. Come on, Michael. We're better than that, aren't we?"

His jaw flexed. His gaze slid to Ali, then back to Greer. "We'll talk about it later," he said brusquely and pushed past them, going inside.

"How do you stand working for him?" Her sister made no effort to lower her voice.

Greer closed her hand around Ali's arm, squeezing as she pulled her farther away from the office. "Michael has a lot on his plate."

"Yeah, Stormy Santiago, from what I hear."

"It's a big case."

"Considering he's sleeping with her, yeah."

Greer dropped her hand from her sister's arm. "What?"

Ali gave her an incredulous look. "Don't tell me you haven't heard the rumors."

"Michael Towers is not sleeping with Stormy Santiago," Greer said under her breath. "He could get disbarred!"

"And maybe he should." Ali's voice was flat. Disregarding the fact that she was jaywalking, Ali set off across the street, leaving Greer to catch up.

"He's also happily married," Greer said when they reached the sidewalk on the other side.

Ali just shook her head. "And I thought Maddie was the naive one. Maybe you're just so busy with your clients that you can't notice what's going on right in your own office." She pulled open the door to Josephine's and gestured. "Age before beauty, dear sister."

Greer went inside, only to stop short at the sight of Ryder sitting in a booth across from a very attractive blonde.

Ali practically bumped into her. But she couldn't fail to notice, either. "*Who* is that?"

"Eliane Dupre," she said in a low voice, steering her sister toward an empty booth on the opposite side of the nearly full restaurant.

"And who is Eliane Dupre?" Ali asked with an exaggerated accent once they were seated. She looked over her shoulder in Ryder's direction.

Maybe the next Mrs. Ryder Wilson.

Greer kept the thought to herself. "Don't stare. They might notice you."

Ali looked back at her and spread her hands. "So?"

"Eliane is interested in the nanny position. She responded to one of the notices I placed for Ryder."

"Ah."

"Mrs. Pyle must be back. Otherwise he'd have Layla with him."

"Too bad. *I* would've loved a chance to see her."

Greer snatched one of the laminated menus out from where they were tucked against the sugar shaker and the bottles of ketchup and hot sauce. It didn't matter that she knew the contents by heart. She still made a point of reading it. Or pretending to read it.

"How's that new baby doing?" Josephine herself said, stopping at the table and without asking, setting glasses of water in front of them before flipping over both of their mugs to slosh steaming coffee into them.

"Liam's perfect," Ali said. Her gaze slid over Greer. "Went over to see them at the hospital yesterday evening. Maddie's supposed to be released today sometime."

"Give her and Linc my best when you see them. You two know what you'd like today?"

"French dip," Ali said immediately. It was pretty much what she always ordered.

"Chef's salad." It was pretty much what Greer always ordered, too. She slid the menu back where it belonged.

"Coming up." Josephine headed back toward the kitchen.

"I suppose that was a dig about me not going to the hospital last night."

"It wasn't a dig. More like a…curiosity. I was there for a few hours. Mom and Dad came by. Vivian. Squire and Gloria Clay. Fortunately, Vivian had already left before they got there. We all sort of just assumed you'd show up after court was through for the day."

Greer grimaced. "I wasn't in court yesterday afternoon. Keith Gowler stepped in for me. Did I tell you that he and Lydia Oakes are getting married?"

Ali wasn't sidetracked. "You took off work? That's the second time this month. You never do that."

"Well, I did. I'll go see Maddie and the baby tonight when they're home." From across the busy diner, she heard a laugh and looked over toward Ryder's booth. His back was to her. But that only meant she had a perfect view of the fair Eliane.

Despite Greer's ripe imagination where the nanny applicant had been concerned, she'd nevertheless pictured someone older. Someone old enough to have left her own country for another. Someone old enough to have a failed marriage under her belt.

But Eliane—with her long, shiny, corn silk–colored hair and perfectly proportioned features—looked no older than Greer.

Younger, even.

"Because of Ryder?"

She belatedly tuned back into Ali. "What?"

Ali turned sideways in the booth. A move clearly designed so that she could look at the man in question without craning her head around.

Greer's lagging brain caught up. "I took off work because of *Layla*," she corrected.

Ali unrolled her knife and fork from the paper napkin. "Sure you did."

"Ali—" She broke off when another musical laugh filtered through the general noisiness of the diner. She exhaled and rubbed her fingertips against her scalp again.

"Having headaches a lot these days?"

"No," she lied.

Ali just watched her.

Greer dropped her hands. The sight of Ryder's booth in her peripheral vision was maddening. "Change seats with me."

Ali's brows disappeared beneath her bangs. But she slid out of the booth and they traded places. Greer pushed Ali's coffee mug over to her and wrapped her fingers around her own. She swallowed. "What if I told you I might have the solution to all of our problems where Layla is concerned?"

Ali mirrored her position: arms resting on the Formica tabletop, hands cupped around her mug. Her voice was just as low as Greer's. "The only problem we have with Layla is Ryder refusing all the offers of help he's gotten from us these past months. The fact that he's still keeping us all at a distance."

"Particularly your husband."

"He *is* her uncle. So what's the solution? Did you find some legal loophole?"

"It's something legal," Greer allowed. "But not a loophole." And she was insane to even be mentioning it to Ali. Much less to think that somewhere along the line, she'd even been giving it the slightest consideration.

"Just cut the mystery, Greer. What?"

Greer exhaled. "Ryder mentioned finding a wife instead of a nanny. You know. For Layla's sake." She took a quick, nervous sip of coffee.

Ali immediately looked toward his booth. "Are you kid—" She broke off when Josephine appeared, carrying their lunch plates.

She started to set down the meals, but stopped. "You switched places. I remember when you used to do that when you were girls, trying to pass for one another."

Ali flicked her streaky hair. "Don't think we'd have much luck on that anymore," she said lightly. "Don't s'pose you have any of that chocolate cream pie left, do you? I thought I'd take a slice home to Grant."

"I'll package one up for you," Josephine promised, and headed off.

"He's buried himself in a new manuscript he started," Ali confided.

"I thought he never intended to write another T. C. Grant book."

"I don't know if it will be another CCT Rules military thriller or not." Ali picked up half of her sandwich. "For all I know, it might be a children's book. I'm just thrilled that he's feeling an urge to write again. As for Ryder—" She broke off, glancing around and lowering her voice. "You think he's going to marry the nanny?"

Greer pressed the tip of her tongue against the back of her teeth for a moment. "Or...someone else," she said huskily. "Me, for instance."

The sandwich dropped right out of Ali's hand, landing on the little cup of au jus and sending it splashing across the table toward Greer.

Greer barely noticed until Ali slapped a napkin over the spill before it dripped onto Greer's lap.

Then her sister sat back on her side of the booth and

stared at her with wide eyes. "How long have you two been…" She trailed off and waved her hand.

"We haven't been." Greer mimicked the wave. She didn't mention the fact that she'd thought about it often enough.

Ali leaned closer. "Yet he *proposed* to you."

"N-not really." He'd been joking. Hadn't he? "But the subject has come up. It would just be a business arrangement," she clarified. "Not a romantic one."

Ali sat back again. She picked up a french fry and pointed it at Greer. "Are you crazy?" She shoved the fry in her mouth.

"Nobody thought the idea was more insane than me." Greer forced herself to pick up her fork and at least look like she was eating. "At first."

"When did all this come up?" Ali waved another fry.

"Last week."

Ali suddenly dropped her french fry and assumed an overly casual smile.

And the back of Greer's neck prickled.

A second later, Ryder was passing their table. He was following Eliane, his hand lightly touching her arm as they progressed through the busy diner. They made a striking couple. Both tall. Both perfect specimens of their gender.

His blue eyes moved over Greer's face and he gave a faint nod.

Heaven help me.

Then he was reaching around Eliane to open the door for her, and they were gone.

Greer's breath leaked out of her. She actually felt shaky.

"Here." Ali pushed a water glass into Greer's hand. "Drink. You look like you're going to pass out."

"I've never passed out and I'm not going to start now." Still, she sucked down half the contents. Then she picked up her fork and jabbed it into her salad, even though the thought of food was vaguely nauseating.

She was well aware of Ali's concern, which was the only reason she was able to swallow the chunk of ham and lettuce. But as soon as had, she set her fork down again. "Layla deserves a mother," she said huskily.

Ali's eyes immediately glistened. "You can't marry someone just because you love a little girl," she said softly.

"Want to bet?" Greer cleared her throat, but it still felt tight. "I also love my sisters. And if I did this, Layla *would* be part of our family. For real. For good. You know I would be able to make certain of it."

"And you? What about you?"

"What about me? I'd be getting the best part of the deal. Layla."

"You know that's not what I mean."

Greer swallowed. "You know I've never thought about the whole marriage thing. My career's been everything."

"Are you sure this isn't *about* your career?" Ali pushed aside her plate of food and leaned her arms on the table again. "Six months ago you told me you were thinking about quitting. Remember that?"

"Trust you to throw a moment of weakness in my face."

But Ali didn't bite. She just sat there, watching Greer, eyes more knowing than Greer wanted them to be.

"It's not about my career," she finally said. "At least I don't think it is. Entirely, anyway."

"Gotta say, Greer. I'm feeling a little freaked out at this indecisive version of you."

"Yeah, well, I'm a little freaked out by the settled-and-married-gonna-have-a-baby version of you. Maddie was one thing. She's had *mama* written all over her since she was playing with dolls. You used to cut off the heads of your dolls and shoot them out of your slingshot."

Ali snorted softly. "I did not."

"Just about. You were both the ultimate tomboy and the ultimate flirt. Everything you want to try your hand at, you succeed at. I'm sure you'll be the same way with motherhood."

"So says Madame Lawyer," Ali said drily. "Maybe I had to try so hard because you've always been the brilliant one. Well. Until now." She spread her palms. "You cannot marry a man you don't love, Greer. Not even for Layla."

"Even if it means solving this problem between Grant and Ryder? I'm at a crossroads here. All I have to do is turn the right way! Maddie's a mom. You're going to be a mom. Well, maybe I want to be one, too!" So what if he'd been joking? He'd been serious enough about the will. She could do a business deal just as well as *Eliane*.

"What happens if you meet someone you really *do* love?"

"I'm thirty years old. It hasn't happened yet."

"You're already talking yourself into it. I can tell."

Maybe she was.

"If you do this, what're you going to tell Mom and Dad? The truth? Or are you going to try making up some story about a sudden romance between the two of you? Because we all know what a rotten liar you are. They'll see right through it. And Mom'll be brokenhearted at the thought of you locked in a loveless marriage."

Greer exhaled. "It wouldn't be like her history with Rosalind's dad."

"She stayed married to Martin Pastore for years because of Rosalind. How's it different?"

"Well, for one thing, Ryder isn't like Martin!" Her encounters with their mother's first husband were mercifully few and far between. "He's not cold and controlling."

"Could've fooled me by the way he's acted for the last six months."

"You don't know him. He's...warm and...and loyal."

"Sounds like a lapdog."

Greer glared.

"Oh, come on. You left yourself wide open for that one."

"You're impossible."

"Admittedly, he's an awful good-looking lapdog. We've grown up around guys in boots and cowboy hats. He does the whole rancher look better than most."

"He does the entire *male* look better than most." She dropped her head into her hands again and massaged her temples. Then she raised her head again and looked at her watch. "I have to get to court."

"You didn't eat anything."

"Trust me. Judge Waters isn't going to care about that." She slid out of the booth. "I appreciate the thought, though." She headed for the door.

Ali followed her, calling out to Josephine that she'd be right back. Then she pursued Greer right out onto the sidewalk. "Promise me you'll think about this a little longer."

A gust of hot wind buffeted the striped awning

over the door and she glanced up, absently noticing the clouds gathering overhead. Maybe the weatherman was finally going to get a prediction right.

"All I've been doing is thinking. Maybe it's time I stopped and just—" She broke off. Shook her head.

"Tossed a coin?"

She managed a faint smile. "Maybe."

Ali grabbed her hands and squeezed them. "Greer, I know what marriage is really supposed to be. I want that for you."

Her throat tightened. "Baby sister, I'll never forgive you if you make me cry now."

Ali made a face.

Greer kissed her cheek and pulled away, checked the street for traffic, and started across.

Ali's voice followed her. "What *did* you do to your feet?"

Greer waved her arm without answering and quickened her pace, trying harder to ignore the tiny cuts she'd gotten from the gravel outside Ryder's house.

She was breathless when she rushed past Bunny Towers sitting at the reception desk and headed straight for her office.

"Oh, Greer. You have some—"

Greer nearly skidded to a halt at the sight of Ryder leaning against her desk. His arms were crossed over his wide chest. He'd set his cowboy hat on the desk beside him.

She swiped her palms down the sides of her black skirt and briskly entered her office, moving around to the opposite side of her desk. "I have to be in court in a few minutes." She started shoving files into her briefcase, heedless of whether or not they were the right ones. "The interview with Eliane went well?"

"She's ready to start tomorrow if I say the word. Didn't even ask about the live-in part. She also agreed to sign an agreement that she'd stay at least six months."

Greer felt a pang in her chest. Who was it that said timing was everything? "I see. Did you tell her about your other idea?"

His eyes narrowed slightly. "You haven't tossed your name in the pool. Does it matter to you?"

She pulled out the will she'd drafted for him and handed it to him. "Not as long as you sign that." Not as long as he didn't decide the lovely Eliane would make a lovely mama and there was no need to plan for disasters.

He tossed the document down onto her desk. "No. I didn't tell her. Yet."

She shoved in a few more files, then hefted the strap over her shoulder. "A live-in nanny's a lot easier to manage than a wife." She edged out from behind her desk again and scooted past him to the door. "I'll cancel the job postings when I finish with court today. Thanks for coming by to tell me."

"I came to bring those, too." He nodded toward the chair sitting inside her doorway and she felt her cheeks turn hot.

Her high-heeled shoes were sitting there.

The same pale gray high-heeled shoes that she'd left in the grass at his place the night before when she'd run out on him like the devil was at her heels.

"Right," she said in a clipped tone. "Thank you. I'm sorry if that took you out of your way."

"Not out of my way. I was in town, anyway."

The clock on the wall above her head seemed to be ticking more loudly than usual. "Did Eliane, uh, remind you of your aunt's model?"

His lips twitched slightly and she wished the floor would open up and swallow her.

"Hey. Didn't expect to catch you."

She whirled to see Ali striding up the hall carrying two plastic bags containing takeout.

"Figured you might as well have your uneaten lunch for—" Ali obviously noticed Ryder then. "Dinner, instead," she finished more slowly. "I'll just stash it in the break room fridge for you. Leave you two to…talk… or whatever."

"No need." Ryder straightened away from the desk and slid his hat in place with a smooth motion. "I was just dropping off those." He pointed at the shoes. "Your sister left 'em behind last night."

Greer cringed even as she saw her sister's gaze drop to the chair.

Ryder's chin dipped a fraction as he thumbed the brim of his hat and turned sideways to go past Greer through the doorway. His arm still managed to brush against hers and she felt hotter inside than ever.

Tick.

Tick.

The clock above Greer sounded louder and louder as Ali slowly looked from the shoes back to Greer.

Her mouth felt dry, which was ridiculous. Ali was her sister. Together with Maddie, they were triplets, for God's sake. "It's not what you're thinking."

Tick.

"Sure," Ali finally said. "Circumstantial evidence, right?"

"Exactly!"

"I think I'm worrying about the wrong thing."

"You don't have to worry about anything, period."

Ali pointed. "You can tell yourself this is about

Layla. And you can tell yourself this is about your job. About being at a crossroads. And I get that it's all true. But if you think you're considering marrying Ryder only because of all that, you're dreaming, big sister. So what happens if you end up actually going through with this, only to realize you're not on the business track at all, but *he* is?"

"That's not going to happen," Greer said flatly. "And it's all semantics, anyway. He's set to offer the job to Eliane."

"The job of wife?"

"Nanny!"

"Are you sure about that?"

Tick.

Chapter Nine

"Templeton! Get your rear end in here."

Greer's shoulders slumped at the command.

She dumped her overstuffed briefcase on her desk and backtracked to Michael Towers's office. *You bellowed?* "Yes?"

"Shut the door."

After her encounters with Ryder and Ali, she'd had a crappy afternoon in court. She'd been late getting to two different arraignments. One of her clients already facing a misdemeanor drug charge got popped with a second offense, meaning she'd lost all the ground she'd made on negotiating a fair plea deal. And she'd gotten into an entirely uncharacteristic argument with Steve Manetti about Anthony Pyle's DUI charge, nearly earning herself a contempt charge.

She closed the door uneasily.

"Sit."

Michael's office was twice the size of hers. Which still meant that there was only room for two chairs. She nudged the one on the right slightly and sat. "If this is about Manetti, I can expl—"

"I warned you to plead out Dilley."

Her lips parted. She swallowed what she'd been going to say about Judge Manetti.

"I tried," she said. "Mr. Dilley refused. He's insistent on having his day in court."

"You have more clients going to trial than any other attorney in my jurisdictions." He was drumming the end of his pencil against his ink blotter. "I think you'd be more effective in Hale's office."

"Hale!" She popped to her feet and the chair wobbled behind her. "He's eighty-five miles away!"

"He's getting ready to retire. You'd be the senior attorney on staff. You could take as many cases as you want to trial."

"Sure. In municipal court." It was the only one located in Lillyette, Wyoming. "Which is in session maybe three times a week. On a busy week. You're punishing me for something. What?"

"I'm not punishing you. I'm trying to promote you."

"By sending me to Lillyette." Braden was a booming metropolis in comparison to the tiny town. "What if I turn down this…kind…promotion?"

Michael stared back at her, unmoving.

Her jaw was so tight it ached. "I see." She aligned the chair neatly where it belonged. She felt blindsided. She'd never lost a job in her life. But she knew that if she didn't accept the reassignment, that was what would happen. "When do you need my decision?"

"End of the week."

She supposed it was better than at the end of this little tête-à-tête. Unable to get out a polite response, she nodded and left his office.

She returned to her own. It was a closet of a space. But whether she'd been feeling frustrated there or not, it had been hers.

Her eyes suddenly burned. Blinking hard, she emptied her briefcase of files and loaded it up for the following day. She scrolled through her email and sent a few brief replies.

Then she shut down the computer, shouldered her briefcase once more and looked up at the clock above the door. As usual, it was a few minutes behind.

She set down her briefcase and moved the chair so she could stand on it to reach the clock. She pulled it off the wall and adjusted the time.

She started to hang it back in place but hesitated. It would just continue to tick along, losing time along the way.

She inhaled deeply and held the clock against her chest as she exhaled.

Tick. Tick.

She climbed off the chair. Moved it back against the wall.

Then she tucked the clock inside her briefcase and left.

Ryder barely heard the knock on his front door above the sound of thunder. The clouds had been building all afternoon. But it hadn't helped with the heat. And aside from the noise, there hadn't been any rain.

The knock sounded again. He closed the logbook he kept on his livestock and went to the door.

Greer stood on his front step.

Her windblown hair gleamed in the porch light. She was still wearing the closely fitted white blouse and black skirt from this afternoon. But she'd unbuttoned a couple of the buttons and rolled up the sleeves. She had bright orange flip-flops on her feet.

And a bottle of whiskey in her hand.

She held it up for his inspection. He looked from the familiar label to her face. It wasn't the finest whiskey on the planet. But in his experience, it did the job pretty well. "Does the occasion call for it?"

"You tell me. I think I quit my job today."

Without asking, she stepped inside, brushing past him.

Another low rumble of thunder rolled through the night. Greer's car, parked on the gravel, was little more than a shadow.

Layla had been asleep for the last few hours. Hopefully she would sleep all the way through to morning, though with the thunder he wasn't going to hold his breath.

He closed the door.

Greer had sat down on one side of his leather couch and propped her feet on the coffee table. The fluorescent orange flip-flops looked more like they belonged on a teenager. But the slender ankles and long calves belonged to a grown woman.

He sat down on the other side of the couch—one full cushion between them—and took the bottle from her. He, too, propped a bare foot on the coffee table. He peeled off the seal on the bottle and pulled out the cork. "Ladies first."

Her dark eyes slid over him as she took the bottle. She lifted it to her lips and took a sip.

He expected a cough. A sputter. Something.

She merely squinted a little, obviously savoring the taste as she swallowed.

When he'd ridden rodeo, the girls had tended toward beer. Daisy had liked a strawberry daiquiri, sweet as hell and topped with hefty swirls of whipped cream. Eliane—the model, not the nanny—had given him his first taste of red wine before Adelaide caught them. Instead of firing Eliane, his aunt had sat down and poured herself a glass, too. Then made him finish the bottle.

To this day, he couldn't drink wine without thinking about that.

It occurred to him now that there was something a little dangerous about being turned on by the way Greer drank a shot of whiskey straight from the bottle.

She handed it to him.

Their fingers brushed. Him, taking. Her, not yet releasing.

"When Daisy first left, I spent a fair amount of time in Jax's company."

Her fingers slid away from his. Away from the bottle. "You must have loved her very much."

"I thought I did. Enough to give her a wedding ring." Just not *the* ring. His grandmother's ring. The one his aunt had kept in safekeeping for him since he'd been a kid. Since she'd taken him in when there was no one else to do so.

He took a drink, squinting a little at the familiar burn and savoring the warmth as it slid down his throat. "Adelaide says I've got a hero complex. That marrying Daisy was more about trying to save her than loving her."

"What do you think?"

He thought about his mother, who'd been just as troubled as his erstwhile bride. He took another drink and handed Greer the bottle.

She cradled it, running her thumb slowly over the

black label. Her nails were short. Neat. No-nonsense. "I've never loved anyone like that," she murmured. "I think it might not be in my makeup."

"Just don't tell me you're a virgin," he muttered.

If he'd thought he would set her off guard, he was mistaken.

She made a dismissive sound. "Sex and love don't have to be the same thing."

"Adelaide would agree."

"I think I'd like your aunt. You talk about her, but you don't talk about anyone else in your family."

"There wasn't anyone else."

Greer studied him for a moment, then looked away. She took another sip. A longer one this time. She tilted her head back a little and her eyelids drifted closed.

He got up and opened the kitchen door. The breeze was finally cooler. He stood in the doorway for a long minute and felt the base of his spine prickle when she came up to stand beside him in her silly orange flip-flops.

"D'you think it'll actually rain?" Her voice was little more than a whisper.

"Finished haying this morning. It can rain for a week straight, as far as I'm concerned."

She pressed her fingertips against the wooden frame of the simple screen door. "Layla?"

"Asleep."

She pushed open the screen door and went outside, taking the whiskey bottle with her. Ryder hadn't turned on the back porch light. Her blouse showed white in the light coming from the kitchen, but the rest of her melted into the darkness.

He caught the door before it could snap shut and followed her out, holding the screen until it sighed silently closed.

He sat on the end of the picnic table, watching the gleam of her blouse moving around as she swished her feet through the grass. Her restlessness was as palpable as the weight of thunder overhead.

"How old are you, Ryder?" Her voice sounded farther away than she appeared.

"Thirty-four." He cupped his hands around the edge of the table. The wood felt rough. It would be full of splinters if he didn't sand it down sometime soon. While he was at it, he could slop a coat of barn-red paint over the whole thing. Cover up all the flowery stuff.

"I'm thirty."

"Are we trading statistics? Want to know my boot size?" He listened to the grass swishing and wasn't sure if it was from her feet or from the breeze. But the gleam of her blouse was getting closer and then she stopped a few feet away from him. "Thirteen."

"Did you give Eliane the word?"

"No."

She took another sip from the bottle, then stepped close enough to set it next to his hip. "Why?"

He moved it down to the bench seat. "Why do you think you quit your job today?"

She started to move again, but he reached out and caught her hands and she went still. Her palms were small. Her long fingers curled down over his. He could see the faint sheen of moisture on her lips.

"Because I don't want to drive eighty-five miles to work every day. Or move eighty-five miles away from my home. Because." She took a step closer. She exhaled a shaky-sounding sigh. "Because."

He let go of her hands and slid his palm behind her neck. Her skin was warm. Silkier even than his imagination had promised. But that was as far as he went.

He didn't pull her forward. Didn't make another single move.

It was one of the hardest attempts at self-control he'd ever made.

"Were you really joking the other day?"

He didn't have to ask what she meant. He didn't have to think about the answer. "No. Are you tossing your name in the pool?"

After a moment she took another step forward and stopped against the edge of the table, between his thighs. When she drew breath, he could feel the press of her breasts against his chest.

"If we do this—" his voice felt like it was coming from somewhere way down inside "—I know what I get out of it. What do you get out of it?"

"Are we talking about marriage?" Her fingertips drifted over his knees, slowly grazing their way higher up his thighs, leaving heat in their wake even through his denim jeans. "Or this?"

He pressed his hands over hers, flattening them. Stilling their progress. "Counselor, I know what you'll get out of *this*."

She leaned closer, bringing with her the seductive scents of warmth and whiskey and woman. The breeze blew over them, and her hair danced against his neck. Her lips brushed against his jaw, slid delicately across his chin. Then she found his mouth for a moment that was strangely endless but much too brief. Her fingers pressed into his thighs. "I get the assurance that Layla will be part of our lives. Permanently. If you want to marry to give her a mother, then I want to *be* her mother. Legally."

He caught her behind the neck again, pulling back so he could see her face. But it was too dark. The sky too black with clouds. Her cheekbones were a faint high-light. Her lips a dark invitation. And her thickly lashed, deep brown eyes…they were the most mysterious abyss of all. "You want to adopt Layla."

"Is that so strange?"

He wasn't sure what it was, except that it made something inside his chest feel strange. "I'll consider it. What else?"

"Our wills. Anything happens to us both, then Layla goes to Grant and Ali. Those are my terms."

"What about starting your own legal firm?"

"Maybe someday when I've won the lottery and can afford it, I'll have one."

He moved his hand along her neck and over her shoulder. The gleam of white fabric looked crisp but did a poor job of hiding the heat radiating from her. "I could stake you."

"It's not just money. An office. Equipment. All that sort of thing. It's time. Time I won't have much of, if I'm out here taking care of Layla."

"You're a lawyer. Your greatest equipment is your brain. And you can turn that fancy-ass Victorian house you're supposedly renovating into an office."

Her hands slid out from beneath his as she stepped back from him. Cool air seemed to flow between them. "You're full of ideas all of a sudden."

"I've given it a thought or two."

"Why does it matter to you? I've already said that Layla is what's important."

"Because I'm never going to be the cause of a woman giving up her dream." He reached for the bottle of whiskey and cradled it in his hand.

She was silent for a moment while the thunder rumbled. "Is this about Daisy?"

"The only dream that Daisy claimed to have was being married to me." He scratched at the edge of the bottle label with his fingernail. "Whatever her real dreams were, she obviously never shared them with me." He figured it was progress that he could make the observation without feeling much of anything.

"What's your dream?"

He spread his arms. "This place."

"The Diamond-L."

"Named for my mother. The original Layla. You want me to talk about her?" He felt the label tear. "She was born here. In Wyoming."

He felt her surprise.

"Her dad—my grandfather—was a minister. Moving his family from one small town to another every few years. They died before I was born. But my mom dreamed of adventure. Of seeing more of the world than a string of tiny towns needing a preacher. Finding the end of the rainbow. And she gave it all up because she got pregnant with a baby she wasn't at all equipped to handle." He took a last burning sip of whiskey before tossing the bottle away into the dark, even though it meant a waste of perfectly good liquor. "She was an alcoholic. One night, she got behind the wheel of a car, drunk, and killed herself as well as two other people."

"Oh, Ryder." Greer's sigh was louder than her words. "How old were you?"

"Eight."

"Your father?"

"She never said who he was."

"And your aunt?"

"Adelaide didn't know who he was, either. She was the only one left to take me in. She's not my real aunt. She was my grandmother's best friend. She was there when my mother lost her mother. And she was there when I lost mine. Adelaide gave me a home." He felt a raindrop on his hand. "I asked her why once. She said it was the right thing to do."

Greer stepped close again and slid her arms around his shoulders. "The Victorian would make a good office," she whispered. "I'll consider it. Put your arms around me."

He didn't need to be told, though it was a novel enough occurrence that it appealed to him. Her waist was so slender, his fingers could span it. But as he slowly ran his hands down over the flare of her hips, he discarded the notion that he'd ever considered her too skinny for his tastes.

"If we do this, it doesn't change anything." She arched slightly when his hands drifted down over her rear. "Layla will have two parents. We'll raise her together. But the deal between us stays—"

"—business." He'd discovered the zipper on the back of her skirt and slowly drew it down. The skirt came loose and slid down her thighs. All she wore beneath was a scrap of lace.

"That's right." She angled her head and brushed her lips against his ear. "Business," she breathed.

He slid his fingers along her slender neck. Felt the pulse throbbing at the base. The way she swallowed when his fingers curled beneath her chin. He nudged at it slightly, lifting it. "You saying this is a one-and-done, Counselor?"

"I'm saying let's not call this marriage something it's not. It'll be a marriage of convenience. Pure and simple."

He lowered his head and slowly rubbed his lips across hers. Felt the softening. The parting. The invitation.

He lifted his head again. Eased his fingers behind the nape of her neck once more. "I'm not thinking too many pure thoughts at the moment."

Her breasts rose and fell, pressing against him. Retreating. "Neither am I. As long as we don't confuse this with something it's not, I don't see the problem. Just because marrying would be convenient doesn't mean it has to be sterile. It'd be a different matter if we weren't attracted to each other. But we are." Her lips were close to his, her whisper soft yet clear. "So we might as well be realistic from the start."

"Realistic. Works for me."

She took a deep breath again. Her breasts pressed against his chest and stayed there. "And…and if…*when* it stops working, when Layla's older, we'll end the deal. No fuss. No muss." She waited a beat. "As long as I'm just as much her legal parent as you. My family—*all* of my family—becomes her family. That means Grant, too."

He felt another plop of warm rain. This time on his arm. "If I agree to you adopting her, you have to agree about your own practice."

"Negotiation?"

"You told me you were good at it."

"Okay. Agreed."

The second she said the words, he closed his hands around her hips again, pulling her in tighter. She was warm. Soft. "It's going to rain."

"As far as I'm concerned, it can rain for a week." He felt her words against his lips.

He smiled slightly and pushed her away. Only a few inches. "Take off your shirt, Counselor."

She made a soft sound. He sensed more than saw her dark eyes on him. "I'd rather you take it off me."

There were invitations to ignore.

There were ones he couldn't.

His fingers brushed against her skin as he found the tiny buttons on her shirt. Impatience raged inside him, but he took his time. One button. Two. All the way down, until it took only a nudge of his fingers and the shirt fell away, too. The bra and panties she wore were as white as the shirt had been. But lacy. Stretchy. No protection at all when he tugged them off.

And then she took a full step backward, giving him enough room to push off the table and pull his shirt over his head. He unfastened his belt and jeans and shoved them down his legs.

Then she crowded close again, slipping her hand under his boxer briefs. She inhaled audibly when she closed her fingers around him. "Perfect," she breathed.

He looked up at the sky, dragging in an audible breath of his own. Another raindrop hit him square on the face. His shoulder. His back. "I should take you inside."

"I'm not sugar." She dragged his briefs down, bending her knees, going down with them, setting them aside when he stepped out of them. But she didn't stand back up. "I'm not the Wicked Witch. I won't melt from some water." Her hair brushed his knee. His thigh. And her lips…

"Maybe not," he said. Her mouth closed over him and he exhaled roughly. He slid his fingers through her hair. He couldn't help himself. She had a lot of hair. The strands were silky. Slippery. He wanted to wrap his fingers in it and hold her. His hands were actually shaking from resisting the urge. "But what you're doing feels damn—" another oath slid through his teeth "—wicked."

The air suddenly felt electric and thunder cracked.

She made a sound. Sexy. Greedy. And took him even deeper.

He let her go. Let her do as she pleased. And oh, how it pleased. For as long as he could hold out. Then a flash of soft light flickered in the distance, giving shape to the canopy of clouds. Giving shape to the woman kneeling before him.

"Enough." It was a rough order. A rough plea. He pulled away. Pulled her up. Maybe it wasn't going to be one-and-done. Maybe they'd manage a year. Two. Before convenience didn't matter to her so much and she'd want more out of life than a business deal of a marriage.

But he wanted more this time—this first time—than just *this*.

Another fat raindrop splashed on his shoulder as he drew her up to him and found her mouth with his. Found her breasts with his hands. And she was right there with him. Pressing herself against him, her nipples tight points against his palms. Her tongue mingling with his, her hands dragging up and down his spine before closing over his head.

He could feel her heart pounding as hard as his own as he lifted her against him. Her legs slid along his thighs and wrapped around his hips. And then she cried out when he slid inside her, and he froze. Because she was so tight. So small in comparison to him, and he was suddenly afraid of hurting her.

Thunder cracked overhead and the clouds finally opened up, drenching them in seconds.

Holding her ought to have been impossible. Water rained down on them, making her flesh slick. But she simply twined herself around him, holding him tightly gloved within. "Don't stop now." She sounded exultant as she dragged his mouth back to hers.

And then everything that was perfect overrode his fear.

Wet inside.

Wet outside.

And she wanted him as much as he wanted her. He backed up until he felt the table. There'd be time for bed later. Time for every other thing he could possibly imagine. He ignored the rough, splintering wood as he leaned against it and took her slight weight in his hands and thrust.

"Yes." She arched in perfect counterpoint.

Again. And again. And again. He wanted to go on and on and on, but he knew he wouldn't last. Not with the way he could feel her quickening. Tightening. Shuddering.

Lightning flashed.

Her head dropped back but she clung to him. "Yes!"

The rain fell and the world shrank down to this one woman in his arms.

And he let himself go.

"Yessssss."

Chapter Ten

"Yes. I do."

Judge Stokes smiled at Ryder and turned to Greer to repeat the vow. "And will you, Greer Templeton, take this man, Ryder Wilson, to be your lawfully wedded husband? To have and to hold, in sickness and in health, for richer or for poorer? Forsaking all others and keeping only to him?"

It was vaguely surreal, standing there in Judge Stokes's chambers.

But there was nothing surreal about Greer's answer. Since she'd made the decision to marry Ryder, she hadn't suffered any second thoughts. "Yes," she said just as clearly as he had. "I do."

The judge smiled benevolently at them. With his white hair and beard, and his tendency toward wearing red shirts, he looked a bit like Santa Claus. Even though it was only the end of August. "Then—" he closed his small black book "—by the authority vested in me by the State of Wyoming, and with a great deal of personal delight I might add, I declare you to be husband and wife." He spread his hands. "Congratulations. You may kiss your bride."

Ryder, looking uncommonly urbane in a dark gray suit with a lighter gray striped tie knotted around his neck, turned to her. He took her hands and his thumb brushed over the narrow platinum band he'd given her. His thick hair was brushed back from his face. There was no hatband mark in evidence. His jaw was clean-shaven and his blue eyes were brilliant. When he leaned down, instead of his usual scent of hay or grass or fresh open air, he smelled faintly woodsy. Exotic.

He was entirely *un*-rancherly.

And for the first time in thirty-six hours—since the night she'd gone to his house and she'd thrown herself, mind and body, into his marriage plan—she felt a wrinkle of unease.

How well did she really know this man to whom she'd just promised herself? This rancher who had a beautiful gray suit that looked as if it had been custom tailored just sitting around in his closet?

Was it a leftover from his Vegas wedding to Daisy?

It was just a suit, she reminded herself. She'd pulled her dress from her closet, too.

Then his eyes met hers, and it felt as though he knew exactly how she was feeling.

"We can do this," he murmured. Low. For her ears only.

She gave a tiny nod.

The faint lines beside his eyes crinkled slightly and his dimple appeared. Then his lips brushed slowly, lightly across hers.

It was barely a kiss. Yet it was still enough to make her feel warm way down inside.

But there was no time to dwell on it, because the judge's wife and his usual clerk, Sue, who were acting as their witnesses, had started clapping. Layla, dressed in a ruffled yellow jumper, jabbered and clapped her hands, too. Sue had insisted on holding her during the ceremony.

"Just lovely," Mrs. Stokes said. "So romantic."

Greer bit back a spurt of amusement that she knew Ryder felt, as well, and relaxed even more.

They were of one mind when it came to that particular element of marriage. They could rock each other's socks off in the bedroom while Layla slept. Or on a picnic table in the rain. Or in his shower that ought to have been too cramped, but wasn't. All of which they'd done in the span of a mere day.

But this legal union of theirs wasn't about romance. It was because of Layla, and for no other reason.

"If I could get your signatures here?" Sue pointed to the marriage license they'd obtained just that morning from the county clerk's office. She evaded Layla's grab for the pen and handed it to Ryder.

He signed the document and handed the pen to Greer before lifting Layla out of Sue's arms. "Thanks."

"My pleasure. It's just so exciting to see a happy ending for all of you."

Greer finished signing her name next to Ryder's and she capped the pen before handing it back. "Thanks, Sue."

"I still can't believe you did this without your family, though. They're going to be so surprised."

"We didn't want anything or anyone—not even family—delaying it," Greer explained smoothly.

"That's how it is, isn't it?" Sue's eyes sparkled. "When you know you absolutely can't spend one more minute without committing to the person you love?"

"It was like that for us, wasn't it, Horvald?" Mrs. Stokes commented as she signed the witness line.

It was easier to let them think that than to tell them the truth. That Greer hadn't wanted to give her family a chance to talk her out of it. Which they would surely have done, no matter how much they, too, loved Layla.

Ryder had disagreed with her. Said they should wait, at least long enough to tell her family. It wasn't about seeking approval or blessings. It was about respecting them enough to give them the truth.

Greer had prevailed, though. They'd made the decision. If they'd waited, they'd have had to wait through Labor Day holiday weekend to be married. Meaning she'd also have to wait four more days to file the petition to adopt Layla.

Sue took up the pen and signed after Mrs. Stokes. Then the court clerk set the document on the judge's desk. "Congratulations again." Sue linked her arm through Mrs. Stokes's and the two of them left the judge's chambers.

"All right." The judge signed the license with a flourish after they'd gone. "I guess I can trust you to turn that in to the recorder's office." He slid the paperwork into its envelope and handed it to Greer. "And now for your next item of business."

He moved another document to the center of his desk. "I've reviewed your petition for Layla's adoption and everything is in order." As he spoke, he signed his name and then he flipped open an enormous date book in which, Greer knew, he kept all of his case schedules. It didn't matter that Sue managed his official calendar by more efficient—namely computerized—methods. Horvald Stokes still liked his old-fashioned calendar. And it was legend how he'd never once made a scheduling mistake.

He flipped through it, studying and muttering to himself under his breath. Then he went back a few pages. Then forward again. And finally he stopped. "Hearing will be November 19." He made the notation in his book and then on the petition. "That's before Thanksgiving."

For the first time that day, Greer's smile felt shaky. Becoming Layla's mother was the crux of the matter, the reason they were there at all. When they were done, Layla would have a father and a mother. The hearing in November would be little more than a formality before Judge Stokes could sign the final decree. "Sounds perfect to me, Your Honor."

"It really is my genuine pleasure." He stood and pulled one of the black robes off the coat stand behind his desk and slipped his arms into the voluminous sleeves. "Layla had a rocky start through no fault of her own. I'm more than pleased that things have resolved themselves in this manner."

A manner that Greer never would have imagined six months ago.

Her throat felt tight. "Thank you again for fitting us into your schedule today."

He winked. "Fifteen minutes for a good cause."

Sue returned then and gathered up both the thick, stapled document that he'd signed and his oversize date book. "Both parties for your next case are present, Judge Stokes, whenever you're ready."

He nodded and she went through the doorway that Greer knew led directly from his chambers into his courtroom. The fact that he zipped up his robe before he headed toward the door meant he was prepared to get straight to business. "Will we be seeing you at the county picnic this weekend?"

Greer moistened her lips and adjusted the band of black velvet fabric around her waist. By itself, her knee-length ivory cotton sundress had seemed a little too casual to wear to her own wedding. Marriage of convenience or not. After seeing Ryder's suit, she was glad she'd made her outfit a bit more formal by adding the wide black belt. The black touches were repeated in the jet clip she'd pinned into her chignon and her black suede pumps.

"I'm afraid not. I've left the public defender's office." She'd turned in her notice to Michael the day before. He'd been livid and told her she needn't serve out the two weeks. Considering the choice he'd given her, she felt like she was the one who had a right to be livid. "I'm cleaning out my desk when we're finished here, actually."

The judge was clearly surprised. "You're not leaving the practice of law, I hope. You're an incredibly valuable part of the legal community, Greer."

The praise was as unexpected as it was touching and she didn't know quite what to say.

"She's opening her own firm," Ryder said.

Greer understood why it was so important to Ryder, even though, in her own mind, it was a much hazier proposition.

The judge's expression cleared. "Good for you! I look forward to you really spreading your wings." His smile broadened. "And one day, Mrs. Wilson," he said, winking, "I'll expect to see you on the bench." He pulled open the door and went into his courtroom.

Which left Greer alone with Ryder.

Her husband.

They'd married so quickly she hadn't even thought whether she was going to take his name. Mrs. Wilson...

Layla was yanking on his tie, jabbering away in her sweet little-girl babble, and Greer pushed away the thought.

"That went smoothly," she said. "Don't you think?"

"It was smooth enough." He tugged at his tie, but Layla looked ready to do battle over it. "I should have said before—you look real pretty."

She dashed her hand quickly down the skirt of her dress, suddenly feeling self-conscious. "I guess the dress did the job. It's ancient. Back from law school days. You...you look very nice, too." She snatched up the small black clutch she'd brought with her, along with the entirely unexpected nosegay of fresh lavender stalks wrapped in gray ribbon that he'd given her. "I guess you must subscribe to the theory that every man should have a decent suit in his closet."

His dimple appeared. "I was afraid it would be a little tight. Last time I put it on was at least five years ago." He looked at Layla, chuckling. "Gonna need a new tie now, though."

So. *Not* the suit from his Vegas wedding.

She lifted the bouquet and inhaled the soothing fragrance. "Looks like it fits you just fine," she managed, and led the way out of the judge's office.

As she clutched the lavender, she noticed how foreign the shining ring felt on her wedding finger. It was a little too loose.

She honestly wasn't sure what had surprised her more. The flowers or the ring.

He'd chosen both. She couldn't imagine when he'd had the time.

She reminded herself that the ring would simply take some getting used to. As would chasing after Layla instead of chasing clients right here among these courtrooms every day.

Simple enough.

They'd reached the wide central staircase. Her high heels clicked on the marble as she started down. It was only ten in the morning. But it was a Friday, which meant that most of the courtrooms weren't in use and the building was pretty empty.

The recorder's office on the first floor was open every weekday, though, and they stopped there to turn in their signed wedding license.

"Don't forget this." The girl working behind the counter was new. She didn't know Greer. She was holding out the certificate portion of the wedding license. Though it was nothing more than a souvenir, the reality suddenly sank in.

Greer's head swam. She took the certificate, feeling embarrassed by the way her fingers visibly trembled. "Thank you." She went to tuck the folded paper in her clutch, but the thick parchment slid out of her grasp. She knelt down to grab it.

When she rose, she swayed.

Ryder's hand closed over her elbow, steadying her. "When's the last time you ate?"

"Yesterday evening." She'd spent the night before at home, wrapping up the details of her resignation. Contacting her former clients and letting them know that she wasn't abandoning them, even though it felt like it. That someone else from her office would be taking good care of them.

She'd fallen asleep in the middle of making case file notes for the attorney who would come after her.

When she'd woken up, she had a crease in her cheek from the folders and a stiff neck from sleeping with her head on her desk. She still felt a little stiff now.

"Let's get you fed, then," he said, caressing her neck, his fingertips somehow magically discerning the tight spots.

"After I clean out my office."

His hand closed around her shoulders. "Your office can wait." Holding her in one arm and Layla in the other, he headed toward the courthouse exit.

"But—"

He didn't slow his long, measured strides. "What's left that matters, Greer? You told me about the clock."

"I don't know," she admitted. "I have stuff there still."

"Paper clips?" They'd reached the courthouse doors and he let go of her to hold one open. "Face it, Counselor. If anything else had truly mattered, you'd have taken it the same time you took the clock."

She hated to admit he was right. "I need to at least drop off the box of files I still have."

"Fine." When they stepped outside, they were greeted by clear blue skies. The heat had broken a little. "*After* you've eaten."

"Is this what being married to you is going to be like? You telling me what's what?" She stopped on the courthouse steps, tucking her clutch beneath her arm and pointing her lavender bouquet at him. Layla was playing with his ear and yanking on his tie as though it was a rein.

"It is when I know I'm right." He tried to smooth his

tie; the attempt seemed futile. He took Greer's hand in his and they began to descend the courthouse steps.

That's when she saw them.

Her parents. Vivian. Her brother and sisters. Their husbands. All of them were there. Even Rosalind, who hadn't visited Braden in years.

Greer yanked her hand from Ryder's. "What did you do?"

"You want Layla to be part of your family. So." He took her hand again, firmly, and nodded toward the not-so-small crowd assembled at the bottom of the stairs. "I called them. Last time I got married it was supposedly for the right reasons. We eloped. Never told a soul until after the fact. And you know how that turned out. So I'm doing things differently this time. I'm not going to pretend we're living in a vacuum. We can't shut out the people who care about us the most." He looked into her eyes, his expression intense. "They're gonna say we didn't marry for the right reasons but I don't care. Our reasons are our own. As long as you and I are on the same page, we're good." He squeezed her hand. "We are good," he repeated. "*Showing* them is the only way they'll get on board."

She moistened her lips. "I'm not so sure I like it when you're right."

He smiled faintly. "You'll get used to it in time."

A fine idea in theory. So why did it make her feel increasingly disconcerted?

Adjustments, Greer.

She tugged his tie away from Layla and smoothed it down the front of his hard chest. Her fingers wanted to linger. Her common sense insisted otherwise. "I guess now I don't have to keep running scenarios in my mind about how to tell my parents."

His dimple appeared. "There you go."

"Have you told Adelaide?"

He smiled slightly. "Who do you think reminded me that a bride should have flowers on her wedding day?"

And just like that, her chest felt tight all over again. "You called my family, but will she come, too?"

He shook his head. "She doesn't travel anymore, remember?"

"Has she met Layla?"

"I had sort of figured I'd visit for Christmas. A few days. Can't spare a lot of time away from the ranch." He was silent for a moment. "We could go. You know. As a family."

"That sounds nice." She lifted her small bouquet and inhaled the lovely, calming scent, though it wasn't quite enough to soothe away the disconcerting butterflies flitting around inside her. "Did she tell you to choose fresh lavender, too?"

"Didn't need to. They were the only flowers that seemed fitting for a woman who lives in a house like yours."

"Lived," she corrected, and looked down at her family. "Well. We can't stand here forever, I suppose. At least they're smiling."

"Yep." He muttered an oath when Layla yanked his tie again. "You're gonna strangle me with it, aren't you, Short-Stuff?"

"I'll take her." Greer handed him her clutch and bouquet, lifted Layla out of his arms and propped her on her hip. Then she took back her bouquet.

He gave her clutch a wry look, then slid it into his pocket. "Ready?"

She nodded.

And they continued down the stairs.

They'd barely made it to the bottom before a collective command came for them to stop where they were. Out came a half dozen cell phones to take their pictures. But then, clearly too excited to wait a second longer, Meredith darted up to greet them, throwing her arms around Greer and Layla, engulfing them in her familiar, uniquely Meredith fragrance.

"Oh, my darlings," she cried, and somehow Greer managed to lose Layla to Meredith in the embrace. But then her mom always had been sly that way. She kissed the baby's face. "You've grown so much! And you!" Meredith dragged Ryder's head down and gave him a smacking kiss on the cheek before he had a hope in heaven of avoiding it. He gave Greer a vaguely startled look. "I knew you were a special man," Meredith was saying, "and when you called us last night, I—"

"Last night!" Greer gave him a look.

"You were home doing your thing. I was doing mine."

Meredith laced her free arm through Ryder's and pulled him the rest of the way down the steps. Since his hand was locked onto Greer's, that meant she went, too, and they didn't stop until they came up against her father's stalwart body. Carter's service in the military might have ended decades earlier, before Greer, Ali and Maddie were even an idea, but he still carried himself as though he wore a uniform and a chest full of medals.

He and Ryder were about the same height. But Ryder's brawny build, hidden so spectacularly beneath his tailored suit, made him seem even larger than her dad.

The men were eyeing each other. Taking measure.

Predictably, her dad went on the offensive. "Guess you didn't figure you needed to call and get permission to marry my daughter before you just did it."

"Dad! I don't need—" Greer broke off when he lifted his hand. She looked to her mother. "Mom."

Meredith just gave her an amused look. She was as unconventional as her husband was conventional, and yet together, they were the perfect couple.

"If I'd done that, and Greer had found out, I'm pretty sure she wouldn't be standing here this morning with my ring on her finger," Ryder replied easily.

"Darn right," Greer started, only to break off again when her dad gave her the same silencing look he'd given all of them growing up.

"The fact that you didn't call for permission makes me feel you know my girl pretty well. The fact that you let us know so we could be here this morning makes me think you've got a few good brain cells."

"Dad!"

"But the fact that my girl chose you, well, that says a lot, too." He looked over at Greer's sisters. "I didn't raise any of my daughters to choose badly. So." He stuck out his hand. "Welcome to the family, son."

It was ridiculous, but Greer's eyes stung a little as her father shook Ryder's hand.

After that, it was pretty much a free-for-all. She wasn't sure if they would have made it from the courthouse steps to Josephine's diner if Ryder hadn't taken charge and made it happen. There was a general jostling for seats and the usual chaos of menus and ordering for such a large party, but the diner was half-empty and nobody else there seemed to mind.

Greer now had stiff competition for Layla's attention. Between Ali and Maddie and her mother fawning, Layla was wholly and delightedly occupied. Linc, with tiny Liam sleeping against his shoulder, was holding his own in a debate about politics with Vivian and Hayley's husband, Seth, who had tiny Keely sleeping against his shoulder. Hayley was trying in vain to change the subject before Carter blew a gasket and jumped into the lively exchange. At the other end of the tables, Rosalind and Archer were giving each other the same fulminating glares they'd always exchanged growing up. Which left Grant. Sitting on the other side of Ryder.

Greer considered offering to switch seats with Ryder, but decided not to. Instead, she just stood up from her own chair and crouched a little, wedging herself in the narrow space between them. A human buffer between her new husband and his former brother-in-law.

The looks she earned from both of them were nearly identical.

She wanted to point that out but knew better. Among her relatives, there was already the likely explosion over politics before too long. She didn't want to chance adding more combustible material because of Ryder's and Grant's mutual grudges.

The fact that Grant had accompanied Ali was promising as far as Greer was concerned, and she gave him a bright smile. "Ali tells me you're working on something new. I think that's great. How's it coming?"

"Fair."

She looked from him to Ryder. Grant's hair was blacker than Ryder's, his blue eyes lighter. Grant had a swimmer's build. Ryder, a linebacker's. Grant was an author who'd already made a fortune several times over with his military thrillers. Ryder was a rancher, whose resources were considerably more modest. They couldn't be more different.

Their only common ground was Layla and the mother who'd abandoned her.

"Ryder was in the army," she said brightly. She rested her hand on his shoulder. "How long were you in?"

He knew what she was trying to do. She could tell. "Four years. Right outta high school."

"And you, Grant?" She glanced at Ryder again. "He served in the air force. That's how he started writing the CCT Rules series. From his experiences there." She looked from Ryder's face to Grant's. "You put in a fair amount of time, didn't—"

"Yoohoo!" The loud greeting came from across the diner and Greer automatically glanced over. Ryder, on the other hand, shoved back his seat with an exclamation and strode toward the tall, gangly woman who'd entered the restaurant.

She had hair dyed black, and turquoise dripping from her ears and her neck and surrounding nearly every finger. A designer dog carrier hung from one skinny shoulder and Greer could hear the yapping of a dog.

There was no question in Greer's mind who the woman was when Ryder swung her right off her feet in a boisterous hug.

No matter what he'd said, Adelaide had still come.

Across the table, Vivian suddenly stood. She was staring at the woman, too. "Oh, my word! That's Adelaide Arians."

"Who the hell's Adelaide Arians?" Grant asked.

"She raised Ryder." Greer had to push the words through the ache in her throat. Across the restaurant, Ryder had set Adelaide back on her feet and she'd handed him something. As Greer watched, he shook his head as if refusing, but then he looked her way and seemed to still.

"She's only considered one of the seminal artists of our age," Vivian was saying as if it were a fact any person should know. "Her work hangs in the Museum of Modern Art! Wyoming and *culture* are simply two different universes," she huffed. "Sometimes I wonder why I bothered coming here." She tugged at the sleeves of her Chanel suit, and the diamonds on her fingers winked.

"Spoken like the snob you are," Carter observed acidly.

"Dad," Hayley started to caution. She was always trying to be the peacemaker between their father and his mother.

"The apple doesn't fall far from the tree, son." Vivian spoke right over her. "You just save your judgment for *me*."

"You are *impossible*!" At the other end of the table, Rosalind had risen from her seat and was glaring at Archer. In turn, he wore the goading expression he always had around her. "Just crawl back under your rock!" Rosalind was practically shrieking.

Liam and Keely were no longer sleeping like little angels against their daddies' shoulders. They both were crying. Which had their mamas jostling to get out of their chairs to resolve the situation.

Layla was banging her sippy cup against the table and joyfully knocking down the towers of plastic creamer containers that Meredith built for her.

And there was Ryder, drawing his aunt up to their table, which had suddenly lost its collective mind. Whatever his aunt had given him was no longer in evidence.

"And this must be her." Adelaide had an unexpectedly booming voice that carried over the bedlam. She gave Greer an appraising look, but there was a glint of humor in her heavily made-up eyes and a smile on her deeply red lips that helped calm the sudden butterflies inside Greer's stomach. "I've got to say, Ryder my boy, your taste has sure improved since that last one."

Grant shoved his chair back and stood. He tossed down his napkin and walked out of the restaurant.

"Oh, dear." Adelaide's voice could have filled an auditorium without need for a microphone. She set the dog carrier on the chair he'd abandoned. "Did I say something wrong?"

Ryder looked at Greer.

She exhaled. "So. Not everything can go as smoothly as it did with the judge."

He frowned. But the lines beside his eyes crinkled slightly and his dimple came out of hiding.

Greer held out her hand toward his aunt. "I'm very pleased to meet you, Ms. Arians. I'm Greer."

"Call me Adelaide," she boomed, and jerked Greer into a nearly bone-crushing hug. "Oh, yes, indeed, the next few months are going to be *great fun!*"

She let go of Greer so suddenly, she had to catch her balance. "You're going to stay for a while, then?"

"Right through Christmas, sugar pie." Adelaide adjusted the eye-popping tie-dyed scarf she wore around her wrinkled neck. "Now where's the little peanut at the center of all these goings-on? Oh, there you are." She strode around the table. "Cute little thing!"

Layla's eyes went round as saucers as she stared warily up at the tall, loud Adelaide. She banged her cup a few times, but without her usual emphatic enthusiasm. Then she opened her mouth and wailed.

Adelaide whipped one of her chunky rings off a finger and waved it in front of Layla. The distraction worked enough to have Layla grabbing the bauble, but not enough to silence her plaintive howling. Adelaide laughed delightedly. "Little thing already knows what she likes and doesn't like!"

"She's gonna put that ring in her mouth," Ryder warned.

"And why not? You used to do that when you were a little mite, too. Stone's the size of a golf ball. She's not gonna choke on it!" She stood there, hands on her skinny hips, and grinned down at Layla.

Greer's arm brushed Ryder's. She was curious about what Adelaide had given him, but figured if he wanted to mention it, he would. Meanwhile, the cacophony around them was only increasing, made worse by the dog's shrill yipping from inside the carrier. She had to raise her voice. "Still think the one-big-family thing is going to be all it's cracked up to be?"

He dropped his arm around her shoulder. "Time'll tell, Counselor. Time'll tell."

Chapter Eleven

"...Happy birthday, dear Layla, happy birthday to you!"

While their party guests finished singing, Greer set the cake she'd gotten from Tabby Clay in front of Layla. It was shaped like an enormous white cupcake with huge swirls of pink frosting on top, and had a single oversize white candle.

"No, no, no," Layla chanted as she looked at the confection facing her. It had become her favorite word of late. Along with "Dadda" and "bye-bye" and "sus-suh," which Greer had figured out was her version of "Short-Stuff." She even had a name for Brutus and Adelaide.

But there had been no more instances of "mama," inadvertent or otherwise.

"Yes, yes, yes," Greer told her, and shooed Brutus away so she could scoot Layla's chair with its booster dulged themselves several times that night. So was it a one-and-done or three-and-done? What was the difference?

There had been no repeat performance.

"Of course she's going to demolish her cake," she assured Grant, blocking the memories as she drew it a little closer to Layla. "This is all yours, sweetie." She pulled one of Layla's fingers through the icing and caught it in her mouth, sucking it off noisily. It was more whipped cream than frosting. "Yum yum."

"Num!" Layla lovingly patted Greer's face. Her green eyes were full of devotion. "Nummy."

Feeling like her heart would burst, Greer pressed a kiss to their toddler's palm. She couldn't keep herself from looking up at Ryder.

He was grinning; he looked dark and piratical with his short, stubbly beard. "Nummy, indeed."

She tried to ignore the heat shimmering through her, but it was futile.

Instead, she turned her focus back to Layla. Camera shutters clicked all around them as she suddenly launched herself toward her cake, squealing with pure, excited delight, sending Brutus into a frenzy of yipping.

It was, Greer decided, a very perfect first birthday for their little girl.

Eventually, though, it was time to clean up the mess.

Not surprisingly, at that exact moment, everyone conveniently found something else to do.

Vivian and Meredith took off in Vivian's ostentatious Rolls-Royce; heaven only knew where or for what purpose. Her grandmother was a terrible driver, but as long as Vivian didn't run her car over something or someone, Greer wasn't going to worry about it. Maddie and Ali were upstairs, giving Layla and Liam a bath. And all of the men, along with Adelaide and the dog, were out checking the cows Ryder had gathered in the big pasture over the last few weeks.

With the dishwasher already full, Greer set herself to the enormous stack of dishes still waiting on the counter and in the sink. She moved them aside, fit the stopper in the drain, squirted dish soap under the running water and got to work.

Overhead, she could hear laughter from the bath and she smiled to herself.

It hadn't been a bad two months since she and Ryder signed their name on that marriage certificate. Moments like this—even elbow-deep in dish water and dirty dishes—were pretty sweet. Ryder had been able to catch up on his nonstop chores and Greer hadn't even missed the PD's office too badly. Particularly once the scandal broke that Michael Towers really was sleeping with their most notorious client, Stormy Santiago. From what Greer had been hearing, nobody from the office was escaping entirely unscathed. There were rumors that a new supervising attorney was going to be brought in from Cheyenne.

Most important of all, though, Layla was thriving.

Greer let out a long breath and turned on the tap to rinse the stockpot she'd just washed.

"That's a big sigh."

She startled, looking over to see Grant closing the kitchen door. "Decide one cow looks pretty much like the next?" she asked.

A smile touched his aquamarine-colored eyes. "Something like that."

She hesitated, wanting to say something, but not knowing what. Instead, she turned back to the stockpot and tipped it upside down on the towel she'd spread on the counter for the clean dishes. "Ali's upstairs. I'm sure Layla and Liam have both had plenty of time in the tub by now."

He didn't head upstairs to retrieve his wife, though. He stopped next to Greer, picked up one of the towels from the pile she'd pulled from the drawer and lifted the stockpot.

"Thanks."

"That was good chili you made. Reminded me of my mom's cooking."

She shoved her hands back into the water. The suds were all but gone. "Thank Adelaide. She supervised. On top of all the other stuff she's done, she wrote a cookbook more than twenty years ago. There are a few used copies still out there. Selling for a ridiculous amount of money online."

"She's something, that aunt of his." He didn't look at her as he ran the towel over the pot. "Whatever comes into her head seems to go right out her mouth."

"At broadcast decibels," Greer added wryly. "I thought at first that maybe she was hard of hearing, but she's not. I think she could hear a pin drop from a mile away. It's just her way."

"Ali says you must be pretty cozy here, all three of you. There are only two bedrooms?"

"Yeah." She rinsed the last pot and handed it to him, then let out the water so she could start with fresh. She had all of the glassware yet to wash. "We've got Layla's crib in with us." More often than not, the toddler ended up in bed with them, usually sprawled sideways and somehow taking up the lion's share of the mattress. Fortunately, Ryder had drawn the line at Brutus coming into the room. Adelaide's rotund pug seemed to think he owned the place now and he'd have been up with them for sure.

"I'm surprised Adelaide didn't take up Vivian's offer to stay with her in Weaver. She's got a lot more space."

"Ryder would sleep on the floor before he'd let Adelaide stay somewhere else. I know she's a bit of a character, but she means a great deal to him. Her coming here at all is major. She doesn't travel." She chanced a quick glance at Grant's profile as she stoppered the sink again and waited for it to fill once more. She knew he'd had a troubled early childhood until he'd been adopted as an adolescent by the same family who'd adopted his sister. "He lost his mother when he was young, too."

"Ali told me."

She turned off the faucet and set a few glasses in the water. "Oh, stuff it," she said under her breath, and angled sideways to look straight at him. "He blames himself, too, Grant. For what happened. Daisy, Karen, whatever name she went by, she was his *wife*. She didn't turn to him any more than she turned to you when she chose to leave her baby with someone else."

He cleared his throat. His jaw looked tight. "I was her big brother a lot longer than she was his wife," he said in a low voice.

"So that means his self-blame is misdemeanor level but yours is felony grade?" She shook her head. "It doesn't work that way, Grant. You must know that. Time is not the measure. You've been married less than a year to my sister. If—God forbid—something happened to her, would your loss be less devastating than mine or Maddie's? We shared our mother's womb."

Heedless of the water still on her hands, she closed her fingers over his arm. "You and Ryder knew your sister in different ways. She didn't tell you everything. She certainly didn't tell him everything. She married him entirely under false pretenses. Whatever your child-hoods were like, as an adult, Daisy did some things that were terribly wrong. I get that she was troubled. I do. But she abandoned her child when she had other op-tions she could have taken! Maybe she regretted it but didn't know how to make it right before it was too late. I know that's what Ali says you believe. And maybe she didn't regret what she'd done at all. Regardless, what she did was what *she* did. What she did not do, *she* did not do. Neither you nor Ryder was her keeper. And you're both losing out, because out of all the people Layla has in her life, the two of you were the ones closest to her real mother!"

Greer's eyes were suddenly burning. "I'm adopting your niece. I don't see how I can possibly love her more than I already do. We can give her an official birthday and a new birth certificate. But one day Layla is going to want to know about her biological mother. Who else is going to be able to give her the answers she needs besides you and Ryder? Seems to me that would be a lot easier if the two of you would stop acting like ad-versaries and start acting like what you are! Two men who cared deeply for the same woman who deeply hurt you both!"

She huffed out a breath and turned to plunge her hands back in the suds. "I'm sorry." The glasses clinked as she grabbed one and started scrubbing it with her dishrag. "I'm sure Ali won't appreciate me sticking my nose into your business."

"As you've just eloquently put it, Karen wasn't only my business." He gently pulled the glass away from her furious scrubbing. "That's quite a closing argument you give." His hand lingered on the glistening glass after he'd rinsed it and turned it upside down onto the cloth. "I just wish things had been different," he said after a moment.

"I'm sure you do." Her eyes were still burning. She couldn't bring herself to say that she wished things had been different, too.

Because if they were different, she believed Ryder would still be with Daisy. Because that was the kind of man he was.

The kind of man who did what was right.

Her stomach suddenly churning, she pulled her hands from the water and hastily dried them. "I'm just going to run up and see what's going on with bath time. The babies must be prunes by now." She hurried out of the kitchen, but instead of heading up the stairs, she bolted for the bathroom behind them and slammed the door shut. She barely made it to the commode in time to lose all of the dinner she'd eaten.

Afterward, feeling breathless and weak, she just sat there on the wood-tiled floor, her head resting against the wall.

It had been two months since she and Ryder had stood in front of Judge Stokes and repeated those simple vows.

It had also been two months since she'd had a period. And this was the fourth time in as many days that she'd lost her cookies after supper.

That little implant in her arm had proven itself to truly be pointless.

She hadn't taken a test. But she knew the truth, anyway.

She was pregnant.

* * *

The house had been quiet for hours since the party when Ryder quietly stepped into the dark bedroom and slid the heavy door shut.

He didn't need a light to see. The moonlight shining through the windows gave him plenty.

He expected to see Layla's crib empty. But there was a bump in one corner: her diapered fanny sticking up in the air.

There was also a bump visible on the far edge of the bed. The sheet and blanket were pulled up high, only leaving visible Greer's gleaming brown hair spread out against the stark white pillow.

He turned away from the sight and exchanged his flannel shirt and jeans for the ragged sweatpants that he'd taken to wearing to bed ever since he'd gotten himself a wife.

The irony wasn't lost on him.

He could say he'd gotten into the habit because his aunt was right there under their roof, snoring away in the second bedroom. He could say it was because they had a toddler in the room.

He could say it.

Couldn't make himself believe it.

He went into the bathroom and quietly closed the door before turning on the light. He brushed his teeth and when he was finished, rubbed his hand down his unshaven jaw. The beard was part laziness, part convenience. It helped keep his face warmer when he was out on horseback gathering cows and the wind was cold and whipping over him.

Mostly, though, it was just his way of being able to face himself in the mirror every morning.

He tossed the soft, plush hand towel over the hook

next to the sink. Somewhere along the way since he'd
married Greer, things like threadbare towels and wrinkled bedding had been replaced by thick terry cloth and
smooth, crisp sheets. There were clean clothes in his
drawers and sprigs of fresh flowers stuck inside glass
jars on the dinner table. And though Greer claimed not
to be much of a cook, Layla had learned there were good
things to eat besides Cow Pie Surprise. Greer hadn't just
kept to the inside of the house, either. The picnic table
he'd intended to sand and repaint had gotten sanded, all
right. Just not by him. And the daisies he'd thought to
cover with red paint, she'd sealed with shellac instead.

Greer's mark was everywhere. Even when it meant
preserving something he hadn't really cared to preserve.

He went back into the bedroom and lowered himself
to his edge of the bed.

It had been two months of nights lying on his side,
one pillow jammed under his neck. Watching her in the
moonlight as she slept on the other edge.

As always, she wore striped pajamas. The kind with
the buttoned top and the pull-on pants. She had them in
yellow. And blue. And red and purple and pink.

The few months that Daisy had been there, she'd
worn slippery satiny lace things or nothing at all. The
bed he'd had then had been smaller. There hadn't been
so much space between them.

He'd gotten rid of the bed.

Gotten rid of the slippery satiny lace things, along
with every other item she'd left behind, except the picnic
table. And he'd only kept that because it was practical.

He'd never figured striped two-piece pajamas were
a particularly sexy thing to wear to bed.

Until he'd spent two months of nights thinking about

reaching across the great divide to unbutton that buttoned top. To slide those pull-on pants off.

Thoughts like that tended to make a long night even longer. So he'd started earlier in the morning with chores. Gone later at night before finishing.

Every square foot of his ranch was benefiting from the extra hours of attention.

Except for the 150 square feet right here in his own bedroom.

He could have made things easier on himself. Could have refrained from insisting Adelaide stay with them even though she'd clearly been interested in taking Vivian up on her offer to stay at her place. The two women couldn't be more different; the one thing they had in common was that they both were uniquely eccentric. Yet they'd hit it off. Ryder knew that big house Vivian had built on the edge of Weaver had more than enough space for a half dozen Adelaides and their pain-in-the-butt pugs.

Yeah, Ryder could have let Adelaide accept Vivian's invitation. If he had, Layla's crib wouldn't be blocking half his dresser drawers. He wouldn't be waking up six nights out of seven to her toddler feet kicking him as she rolled around in her sleep, unfettered in the space between Ryder's edge of the bed and Greer's because she wasn't even sleeping in her crib.

It was his own fault.

The night of their courtroom wedding, he should have pulled Greer across the mattress. Should have met her halfway.

He should have started as he meant to continue. Should have given her his grandmother's wedding ring that Adelaide had produced when she'd shown up so unexpectedly on their wedding day. Should have made love with her on their wedding night.

But he hadn't. And he was damned if he knew why.

The ring was sitting in its box inside the dresser half-blocked by Layla's crib.

And here they were.

As far apart as humanly possible on a king-size bed.

He lifted his head, rebunched the pillow and turned to face the saddle propped on the saddletree. If he moved the damn thing to the tack room where it belonged, there'd be room for the crib there instead.

But he was proud of that saddle. He'd won it at the National Finals the last year he'd competed. The same year he'd won the money that he'd kept so carefully in savings because ranching was never a sure thing and he'd wanted to be certain he had enough to carry him when times were lean.

The money that he was dipping into now just to make sure his wife from the other edge of the bed had a place to hang her legal shingle that didn't have rotting floorboards and dicey electrical wiring.

Two minutes later, cursing inside his head, he turned over again to stare at his sleeping wife's back.

Only she'd turned, too.

And she wasn't asleep.

And so there they lay. Facing each other across the great divide. Her eyes were dark pools of mystery.

Finally, she whispered, "What are you thinking?"

He cast around for something to say. "It was a nice party."

"Mm." She shifted a little. "Even after Brutus jumped on the counter to eat the leftover cake." She tucked her hands beneath her cheek in the same manner as Ade-

laide's angels from her ceramic phase. "Can I ask you
a question?"

She was still whispering. Probably didn't need to. At
least not for Layla's sake. Lately, the baby had been able
to sleep through anything. Not even Adelaide's booming voice disturbed her anymore.

"What?"

"Why didn't you want to do the paternity test?"

Of all the things she might have asked, that was the
last thing he expected.

She shifted again, and for half a moment, he thought
maybe she was shifting closer. An inch. Even two.

But no. Nearly an entire mattress still lay between
them.

"What purpose would it have served? Soon as I
learned her name, I knew I was going to take her."

"But don't you want to *know*?"

"Have it confirmed that on top of everything, she
cheated on me?"

"It might confirm that she didn't."

"And which is worse?"

Greer didn't respond to that. She turned her head
slightly and he knew she was looking toward the crib.
At Layla inside it. "Are you afraid it will change how
you feel about her?"

"No."

"Are you lying?"

He thought about not answering. But there was
enough distance between them just from the gulf of
mattress. "Maybe." He wasn't proud of it. "She's mine.
Ours," he corrected before she could. The adoption
wasn't yet final, but it might as well have been. "I don't
want what the DNA test says to matter, and that is more
about Layla's mother than it is about Layla."

Greer was silent for so long, he thought maybe she was simply going to turn over once more. Turn her back to him. But she didn't. "Do you still love her?" she finally asked in her hushed voice.

"No. And you don't have to ask if I'm lying. The answer's no." On that his head was clear. He wished it were as clear when it came to the woman lying across from him.

"There might come a day when Layla wants to know."

He knew she meant about the DNA. "That's another matter." He'd given it some thought. "I already have a DNA profile. If it ever comes time to use it, it'll be waiting."

She pushed up onto her elbow, obviously surprised. Her hair had grown since they'd said "I do." It curled around her shoulders now. Softer. Lusher. It was almost as unfamiliar as his beard. "You do?"

"That last year I was bronc bustin'." He pushed up onto his elbow, too, and nodded his head toward the saddle behind him. "When I won that. I was served with a paternity suit. The girl was looking for a piece of my winnings. She thought I'd just let her take it. But I knew it was bull. I'd slept with her, but that baby wasn't mine. Test proved it."

"But Layla's different?"

"Layla had no one else. She was my wife's child."

She lowered herself back down off her elbow with her hands tucked beneath her chin. "So it was the right thing to do," she whispered.

He lay back down, too. Bunched the pillow beneath his neck. There was no need to answer, but he did. "Yes."

She exhaled softly. Leaving him wondering what she was thinking.

All he had to do was ask.

All he had to do was stretch his arm toward her. Offer his hand.

It wasn't too late to break the habit of two months of long nights. The great divide could be breached. Could be destroyed.

All it would take was a step.

He shifted and in the moonlight he could see the way she tensed.

He lifted his head, rebunched his pillow and closed his eyes.

Chapter Twelve

"Happy Thanksgiving!"

Greer smiled at her mom as she walked into the house where she'd grown up. Layla was walking at her side. Her steps were the sweet, plopping sort of steps that all toddlers took at first. She had one hand clasped in Greer's, the other in Ryder's. "Happy Thanksgiving. Smells great in here."

Despite the bare, frozen ground outside, the house was warm. Greer noticed Meredith's feet were typically bare as she hurried out of the kitchen and across the foyer to give them a hug. The tiny bells around her ankle jingled and Layla immediately crouched down, trying to catch them. "Bell," she said clearly.

"That's right, darling. Grandma's bells." Meredith scooped up the baby and nuzzled her nose. Layla's rosy-gold hair would probably never be as thick as Greer's mom's, but it might turn out to be just as curly. "Did you get it?"

Greer held up the envelope she was carrying. "It's official. I picked up our copy of the final adoption decree yesterday just before the recorder's office closed for the holiday." She pulled out the document and handed to her mother.

"Well." Meredith was teary as she paged through it before setting it on the entryway table. Her gaze shifted from Ryder to Greer. "Congratulations, Mommy."

If they only knew.

Greer blinked back the moisture in her own eyes. She glanced at Ryder and quickly looked away. She still hadn't told him that she was pregnant. She hadn't told anyone, except her doctor.

"It's a fabulous day," Adelaide practically shouted in greeting, coming inside behind them. She was carrying Brutus inside his expensive leather transport. "Meredith, I've decided I need to photograph you."

Her mom's eyebrows flew up. "Whatever for, Adelaide?"

"Just be glad she's out of her nude phase," Ryder commented drily.

He was still wearing the closely cut beard he'd started before Layla's birthday. Now the stubble was full-on beard. Still short. Still groomed. But his dimple was hidden.

"She'd still be a fine-looking nude," Carter said as he walked past. He was carrying two bottles of beer and handed one to Ryder.

"Dad!"

Meredith was smiling, though, and the look that passed between her parents was almost too intimate to bear.

"Pardon me while I go throw up," she muttered for effect as she walked around them and headed into the kitchen. Her mother's laughter followed her.

Fortunately, Greer's after-dinner morning sickness had faded. Unfortunately, she knew she was going to have to fess up sooner rather than later to everyone— her husband most particularly. So far, she hadn't even let her belt out a notch; her stomach was as flat as ever. The obstetrician she'd sneaked over to Weaver to see had needlessly reminded her it wasn't going to be long, though. When Maddie was carrying Liam, she'd been visibly pregnant at four months. Same with Ali, who was now six months along.

Greer could either admit the truth in the next few weeks, or she'd be showing it, if her sisters were anything to go by.

But that didn't mean she was going to worry about the fallout today.

Not when it was Thanksgiving. Not when she felt positively ravenous and there was a veritable feast for the taking.

Every inch of kitchen counter was covered with trays of food. She grazed along, plucking olives and candied pecans with equal enthusiasm. Within minutes, she could hear more people arriving. More family members. More friends. Even Vivian, despite the ongoing animosity between her and Greer's dad and uncle. And soon the house was bulging at the seams.

There was laughter and squabbling and it was all dear and familiar. And despite the secret she harbored, Greer felt herself relax. Even when she and Ryder were sitting so close to each other at the crowded table that the length of his strong thigh burned against hers, and they couldn't lift their forks without brushing against each other.

After the glorious feast, it was football. The options were to watch it on television or play it on the winter-dead front yard, where Archer was warming up, tossing the football around with their cousins and their brothers-in-law.

Ali intercepted the ball and looked toward her sisters and their cousins. "Guys against the girls? Cousins against cousins? What'd we do last year?"

"Cousins," Maddie reminded her with a laugh. "And it was a slaughter."

"Only because Seth turned out to be a ringer." Quinn was the eldest of their cousins and, like Archer, had only sisters. "I say Templetons against the spouses!"

His wife, Penny, rubbed her hands together and laughed. "I'm game for that. Means I've got nearly all the guys on my side!"

Ali looked toward Greer where she stood on the side-lines.

"Count me out," Greer said hastily. She had her hands tucked into her armpits and was stomping her feet to keep them warm. The snow in October had been a onetime occurrence and melted away, but the temperatures had hovered around freezing ever since. "It's too cold!"

"What a wuss you've become," Ali chided with a laugh. "Go find Maddie, then. And Ryder. It's his first Thanksgiving game, same as Grant and Linc." Her smile was devilish. "Gotta initiate these men of ours into the family just right." She tossed the ball from one bare hand to her other. "Rules are same as always. No tackle. Just touch."

"Think you've been touched enough," Archer called

to her. "Don't know what's bigger, that football or your belly."

Ali preened, tucking the ball under her arm as she framed her bulging bump against the Green Bay sweat-shirt she wore in honor of their father's favorite team.

Then Grant, the guy responsible for her baby bump, came up behind her, poked the ball free, and the game was on in earnest even though the teams weren't en-tirely present and accounted for.

But that was always how it went.

The most basic rule of Templeton Family Football was for everyone to have fun. The second basic rule was for everyone to stay out of the hospital.

Greer was smiling as she went back inside. She found Maddie in the study, nursing Liam while she ate another piece of pumpkin pie with her fingers. Greer let her be and went to find Ryder. He wasn't in the family room, where her dad and uncle were sprawled out in front of the large-screen television. Nor in the kitchen, where her mom and aunt were still cleaning up the dishes.

"Have you seen Ryder?"

Meredith pointed toward the screened sunporch off the kitchen. Beyond that, Greer could see him and Ad-elaide sitting outside on the park-style bench in the mid-dle of the flower garden. Right now, the only flowers in view were the brightly painted metal ones that were planted in the ground on long metal spikes. Layla was chasing after Brutus as he ran around the yard sniffing every blade of dead grass.

Greer smiled at the picture they all made and opened the kitchen door, going out to the sunporch. She peeled back a corner of the thick clear plastic that her dad hung up in the screened openings so that Meredith could enjoy the space whether it was cold or not. "Ry—"

"Why haven't you?" From all the way across the yard, Adelaide's voice wasn't quite megaphone-ish, but it was still audible.

Something about the tone made Greer swallow the rest of her husband's name.

"It's my decision, Adelaide." Ryder's voice was much quieter. Underlaid with steel.

Disquiet slithered down her spine. One part of her urged retreat. The other part refused. Morbid curiosity kept her pinned to the spot, prepared to witness disaster.

"If I wanted to give her the ring, I would have."

"It's a mistake, Ryder."

Oblivious to their audience, Ryder shoved off the filigreed bench. "Consider it one more mistake I've made when it comes to marriage." He whistled sharply. "Brutus. No." The dog had started digging near the base of a tree. His words had no effect on the little dog. "Adelaide—"

"Brutus, come." At least the pug sometimes listened to his mistress. The dog retreated and hopped up onto Adelaide's lap.

Ryder swung Layla up high and she laughed merrily, sinking her hands into his hair when he put her on his shoulders as he headed in Greer's direction.

Closer. Closer.

She exhaled, finally managing to drag her mired feet free as she hurried back into the house before he could see her.

She caught the glance her mother gave her as she scurried through the kitchen. "Cold out there," she said a little too loudly.

"Your dad's got a fire going—"

Greer waved her hand in acknowledgment as she

fairly skidded around the corner and escaped into the hallway by the front door.

She sucked in a breath, pressing her palm against her belly, knowing she had to keep it together even though inside she felt like she was unraveling.

Ryder never said what he didn't mean.

No matter what he'd said the day they got married, he obviously considered the business of *their* marriage as one more mistake.

"There you are." The man in her thoughts rounded the corner of the hallway and she froze. Layla was no longer on his shoulders. "Adelaide's getting pretty tired. I thought I'd run her back to the ranch."

"I can do it," she heard herself offer. "Layla's going to need her bath and bed soon, anyway. Your…your presence is wanted on the football field."

Even as she said the words, the front door flew open and Grant rushed in. His hair was windblown, his cheeks ruddy. "Tell me you played football."

Ryder's eyes narrowed slightly. "Running back, but not since high school. Helluva while ago."

Grant beckoned. "Better'n nothing." He looked at Greer. "I'm pretty sure we've been sandbagged. Ar-cher—"

Any other day, Greer would have enjoyed the moment. "All-state quarterback."

"And my wife? What was she? All-state sneak?"

"Track. All three of us." She spread her hands, managing a smile even though it felt as brittle as her insides. "We grew up on football. Dad didn't care whether we were girls and more interested in horses and ballet or not."

"Should've known." Grant turned to Ryder. "We spouses lose this game and you know it's gonna follow us the rest of our married lives." He clapped his hand over Ryder's shoulder. "It's a matter of pride."

Ryder looked her way.

"It's a matter of pride," she parroted. "Vivian'll give you a ride home. I'm sure she'd be happy to detour to the ranch on her way back to Weaver."

"She'd be happy, but I've seen her drive." Still, he was smiling a little as he went out the door with Grant.

As if all was right.

As if it mattered to him that losing this first game might seal his fate for all their Thanksgiving football games to come.

She looked out at the two of them jogging out to join the scrimmage. She called after them. "Just remember, no tackling!" If her voice sounded thick, it didn't matter.

She was the only one who noticed.

She closed the door.

The adoption decree was sitting on the table against the opposite wall. She picked it up and slid it carefully back into its envelope.

Then she went to retrieve her daughter and Adelaide and her yapping dog, and they went home.

She was glad that all of her passengers fell asleep on the way.

It meant that they never saw the tears sliding silently down her cheeks.

"Here." Ali handed Greer a hanger. "Try that one."

Greer slid the red tunic off the hanger and pulled it over her head. It hung past her hips over her long black palazzo pants She turned sideways to view herself in the full-length mirror.

The small bulge of her abdomen was disguised among the ridges of the cable knit.

She exhaled. "Okay. This one'll work." She dashed her fingers through her hair. She hadn't had it cut in months. Not since she'd left the PD's office. With the help of her prenatal vitamins, it was growing even faster than usual. It was already down to her shoulder blades.

Unfortunately, her good hair days weren't making up for all that was wrong.

Ali just shook her head, looking decidedly Buddha-like as she sat cross-legged on the counter in Greer's bathroom at the Victorian. "You should've told him by now, Greer."

"I will." She lifted her chin as she peered into the mirror and applied some blush so that her face wouldn't look quite so washed out against the brilliant vermilion tunic. "Adelaide is leaving the day after Christmas. I'll tell him about the baby after she's gone. That's only four days from now."

Ali folded her hands atop her round belly. While Greer was hiding the changes in her body, her sister was delighting in showing off hers. At that moment, she wore a clingy white sweater and burgundy leggings that outlined every lush curve she'd developed.

And why not?

Ali and Grant were besotted with each other. She had no reason whatsoever to want to hide what that love had produced.

It was Greer's bad luck that she'd somehow fallen in love with her own husband. She knew when he learned about the baby, she wouldn't be just another mark in his column of marital mistakes. She—and their baby—would become his next "right thing to do."

And it was almost more than she could bear.

She didn't want to be his responsibility. And she

didn't want to be his business partner in this sterile marriage.

"I still can't believe Ryder hasn't noticed," Ali was saying. "Maybe you can hide that bump under thick sweaters and shapeless pajamas, but your boobs are another story. Is the guy blind?"

Greer tossed the blush in the vanity drawer and pulled out the mascara. They'd met at the Victorian— which was still undergoing renovations—to finish wrapping the Christmas gifts they'd been stashing away there, before heading over to Maddie and Linc's place. They were hosting a party for his employees at Swift Oil.

Grant was waiting downstairs in what was originally the living room, but was now a framework for a reception area and two offices.

Ryder hadn't come at all. He'd been moving the bulls to their new pasture that day and the task was taking longer than he'd planned.

Greer suspected he was just as relieved as she was that he had a valid reason to miss the party.

"He doesn't have to be blind when he doesn't look to begin with." Her voice was flat.

"I don't know." Her sister was unconvinced. "You guys still share a bed."

Greer cursed softly when she smudged her mascara. "A bed where he stays on his side and I stay on mine. And never the twain shall meet."

"Seems to me you could twain your way over to him if you wanted to. You did it before. That's how you got yourself in the family way."

Greer ignored that as she snatched a tissue from the box next to Ali's knee and dabbed away the mess she'd made.

It was too bad she couldn't dab away the mess of her marriage with a simple swipe.

"I should have never confided in you in the first place," she told her. Not about the rainstorm. Definitely not about the great divide that existed between her side of the bed and his.

"I think you needed to tell somebody," Ali said quietly. Her eyes were sympathetic. Ali was always easier to take when she was full of sass and vinegar than when she wasn't.

Greer cleared her throat as she balled up the tissue and tossed it in the trash. "You just happened to catch me in a bad moment."

"Sure. Sitting on the side of the road near Devil's Crossing bawling your eyes out. A little more than a bad moment in my view, but if that's what you want to call it."

She'd been on her way back from an appointment with her obstetrician in Weaver. She'd started blubbering near the spot where Ryder had rescued her that day in August, which now felt so long ago. She had pulled off the road before she ran off it. Ali, in her patrol car, had spotted her. And the entire story had come pouring out of Greer, along with her hiccupping sobs.

"Hormones." Finished with the mascara, Greer capped the tube and tossed it next to the blush, then shut the drawer with a slap. "I'm ready." She tugged her pants hem from beneath her high heel where it had caught.

"More like a broken heart," her sister was muttering under her breath as she unfolded her legs and slid off the counter. "I warned you that something like this would happen." She followed Greer through the bedroom and downstairs.

While Greer didn't appreciate the "I told you so," she did appreciate Ali's return to form.

"Finally," Grant said when he spotted them. "Sooner we get to this deal, sooner we can leave. We're already going to be late."

"Party animal," Ali joked. She lifted her hair when he helped her on with her coat.

Grant's smile was slanted. "I'll party your socks off when we get home."

"Well, now, that *is* a good reason to get moving along."

Greer grabbed her coat and headed out the door. She didn't begrudge her sister's happiness. Truly, she didn't. But her hormones were at work again, and she really didn't want to have to go back upstairs and redo her mascara again.

She paused on the front porch as she pulled on her coat. Every house down the hill from the Victorian was outlined in bright Christmas lights. There still hadn't been any snow since October, but it was pretty all the same.

At the ranch, Ryder had put up the Christmas tree he'd cut down himself. He'd left the decorating of it to Greer and Adelaide, though. The results had been interesting, to say the least. Adelaide's unusual eye might be highly regarded at MoMA, but Greer was probably a little too traditional to fully appreciate the strange paper clip–shaped objects juxtaposed with the popcorn garland she was used to.

She stifled a sigh, climbed behind the wheel of her car and pulled away from the curb. Ali and Grant were in their SUV behind her. She'd become accustomed to using Ryder's truck, because Layla's car seat fit so much better into it. But Layla was back at the ranch with Adelaide. Ryder's aunt had declined the invitation, saying that two parties within just a few days of each other were more than she was used to. And Vivian's annual fete was the night after next on Christmas Eve.

Greer wondered if Ryder would find an excuse to miss that party, too. If he did, it was going to be a little harder for her to explain away his absence. Her brother-in-law's company party was one thing. Vivian's, quite another.

As Grant had predicted, the party was in full swing when they arrived at the Swift mansion.

Greer left her coat in the foyer with the teenager who'd been hired to handle them and aimed straight for the bar. She longed for a cocktail, but made do with cranberry juice and lime. Then she filled a small plate with brownies that she knew Maddie had made from scratch and a half dozen other little morsels.

If anyone did notice her bump, they'd just figure it was from gorging herself.

Christmas music was playing in the background, loud enough to cover awkward silences as employees settled in but not so loud that it was annoying. If Vivian held true to form for *her* party, she'd have a live quartet. When it came to her grandmother, expense was no object. She imported the musicians from wherever she needed to.

Greer wandered through the house, smiling and greeting those she knew as if she wouldn't want to be anywhere else. There wasn't a corner or a banister that hadn't been decked with garland and holly, and the tree that stood in the curve of the staircase was covered in pretty red-and-gold ornaments. She stood admiring it, sipping her juice.

"Looks a little more like a normal tree than ours."

Greer jerked, splashing cranberry juice against her sweater. She blotted the spot with her cocktail napkin and stared at Ryder. "I thought you weren't coming." He was wearing an off-white henley with his jeans, and it just wasn't fair that he should look so good when she felt so bad.

"I thought I wasn't." He shrugged. "But I got the bulls settled finally and decided to come." His blue eyes roved over her face, but they didn't give a clue to what he was thinking. They might be married, but she felt like she knew him no better than she had when they'd first met.

He took the napkin from her, folded it over and pressed it against her sweater. "Would you have preferred I hadn't?"

Her heart felt like it was beating unevenly and she hoped he couldn't feel it, too. "Of course not," she managed smoothly. "You just surprised me, that's all." She tugged the napkin away from him and crumpled it. "There's a bar and an entire spread." She gestured with the hand holding her plate of food. "You should go help yourself. Maddie's brownies will go fast."

His gaze seemed to rest on her face again for a moment too long before he headed off.

She blamed the impression on her guilty conscience.

No matter how strained things were between them, she knew she needed to tell him about the baby.

This time, there'd be no room for him to doubt the paternity. It was the only positive note that she could think of in what felt like an intolerable situation.

"That you, Greer?"

She looked away from watching Ryder to see a familiar face. "Judge Manetti!"

He smiled. "It used to be Steve, remember? We're

not in my courtroom now." He leaned over and kissed her cheek. "When I saw you at first, I thought you were Maddie." He waved his fingers. "The hair's longer. You're looking good. Heard you got married. It must suit you."

She kept her smile in place. It took an effort, but she'd had a lot of practice. "I didn't know you were part of Swift Oil."

"My wife started there a few months ago." He looked around the room. "Always wondered what it was like inside this old mansion. Pretty impressive."

It was a little easier to smile at that. "I think so, too. How're things over at civic plaza?"

"Crazy. You know about—" He broke off and nodded. "Of course you know about it. Heard they've got a short list for the top spot in your old office."

From the corner of her eye, she saw Ryder returning. "Oh? Someone from Cheyenne, I suppose."

He shook his head. "You really don't know?"

"I really don't—ah. Keith Gowler? He's got the trial experience. I think he's pretty happy being in private practice, though. Means he can take cases for PD when he chooses."

"Not Keith. You."

She blinked, then shook her head. "No. Not possible. There're too many other attorneys in line ahead of me. And I quit, remember?"

Ryder stopped next to her and set his hand against the small of her back. She nearly spilled her drink again. "Friend of yours?"

She turned and set the cranberry juice on the edge of a stair tread at the level of her head, along with her still-full plate. "This is Judge Steve Manetti," she introduced. "Steve, my...my—"

"Ryder Wilson." He stuck out his hand. In comparison to Steve's, his was large. Square. A working man's hand.

She moistened her lips, reminding herself to keep a friendly smile in place. "Steve and I have known each other since elementary school."

"I was just telling your wife that she's on the short list for replacing Towers."

Ryder's brow furrowed. "She's opening her own practice."

"No kidding!" Steve gave her a surprised look. "I hadn't heard that. Not that you wouldn't be great at it, but I always thought you had the public defender's office running in your veins."

"Guess not," Ryder answered before she could. His fingers curled against her spine. "If you'll excuse us, there's someone we need to see."

The judge smiled as Ryder ushered her away, but Greer recognized the speculation in his gaze. As soon as they were out of earshot, though, she jerked away from Ryder. "I didn't know caveman was your style. What was that all about?"

"You're not going to work for the PD office again."

She felt her eyebrows shoot up her forehead. "First of all, I haven't heard this short-list rumor. And second of all, even if I had, I would think that's my decision, wouldn't you?"

"Working in that office ran you ragged. And that's when you were an expendable peon."

She stiffened. "Good to know you had such respect for the work I did there!"

His lips tightened. "That's not what I meant and you know it."

She propped her hands on her hips and angled her

head, looking up at him. "No, I don't know it. Why don't you explain it to me?"

"You really want to run that place? What about Layla? Months ago, you told me she was what was important and I believed you. Who's going to take care of *our daughter* when you're spending eighty hours a week defending drunk drivers and shoplifters?"

She gaped. "If that's the way you feel, why on earth did you ever insist on my opening my own practice? And don't go on about it being my *dream*! You think I'd be able to grow a practice from scratch with Layla on my hip 24/7?"

"You'd be calling your own shots," he said through his teeth. "Controlling your own schedule. You'd still have time to be a mother. Or now that you've finally got that right legally, has it lost the luster? You want to dump her off on someone else while you go off to do your own thing?"

She could barely form words for the fury building in her. She was literally seeing red. "You can regret marrying me." Her fingers curled into fists as she pushed past him. "But don't you *ever* compare me to Daisy."

He caught her arm. "Where are you going?"

She yanked free. "Away from you."

The foyer had become a traffic jam of people arriving at the party. Greer veered away and started up the staircase instead.

"Dammit, Greer." He was on her heel. As unconcerned as she was that they'd begun drawing attention. He closed his hand over her shoulder and she lost it.

Quite. Simply. Lost it.

She whirled on him. *"Don't touch me!"*

He swore and started to reach for her again.

That he kept doing so now infuriated her, when he

hadn't reached for her at all in the way that mattered most ever since they'd been married. She swatted his hands away, taking another step. But her heel caught again in the long hem of her pants and she stumbled. She steadied herself, though, grabbing the banister, and blindly took another step.

Right into the plate that she'd set on one of the treads. Her shoe slid through brownies and ranch dressing and she felt herself falling backward, arms flailing. Some part of her mind heard someone gasp. Another part saw Ryder's blue eyes as he tried to catch her.

And then she landed on her back and bounced against the banister so hard the Christmas tree next to the staircase rocked.

And then she saw no more.

Chapter Thirteen

"How is she?"

From the hard plastic chair he'd been camped in, Ryder lifted his head and looked from Meredith and Carter to Greer. She was lying asleep in the hospital bed. The white bandage on her forehead was partially hidden by her hair. The rest of the damage from her fall was harder to see. Harder to predict.

Which was why she was still lying in the hospital bed at all thirty-six hours later.

His jaw ached. "She hasn't lost the baby." *Yet.* He didn't say that part. But it felt like the word echoed around the small curtained-off area all the same.

He still was trying to resolve the fact that he'd learned she was carrying his child at the same time he'd learned she was very much in danger of losing it.

Now his wife was being carefully sedated while they waited.

Meredith's hand shook as she pressed it to her mouth.

"She's going to be all right," Carter told her, kissing her forehead. His arm was around her shoulder. "Nothing is going to happen to our girl on Christmas Eve."

Ryder wished he were so convinced.

Meredith finally lowered her hand. "Where's Layla?"

"Ali picked her up this morning." Much as he loved Adelaide, she wasn't up to the task of keeping up with an active one-year-old for more than a few hours at a time.

"That's good." Meredith nodded. She scooted past Ryder's legs until she reached the head of the bed, and then dropped a tender kiss on her daughter's forehead.

Ryder looked away, pinching the bridge of his nose.

"Have you gotten any sleep?" That was from Carter.

He shook his head. How could he sleep? Every time he closed his eyes, he saw Greer tumbling backward down those stairs.

"Maybe you should."

He shook his head.

"At least take a break."

He shook his head.

Carter stopped making suggestions. He sighed and squeezed Ryder's shoulder. "She's going to be all right, son. If the baby—" He broke off and cleared his throat. "I know you don't want to hear it. But there can be other babies."

But Ryder knew otherwise. This baby was their only chance. Greer was never going to forgive him no matter what happened. He was never going to forgive himself.

He propped his elbows on his knees again and stared at the floor.

Eventually, Meredith and Carter left with promises to

return later. They'd bring him something to eat. They'd bring him something to drink.

It didn't really matter to him.

The only thing that did was lying in a hospital bed.

Inevitably, more family members visited. Hayley. Archer. Cousins he knew. Cousins he didn't.

Nobody stayed long. There wasn't space for more than the one chair Ryder was occupying. And he was too selfish to give up his spot by Greer's bed, even to all the other people who loved her, too. Finally, he must have dozed off. But he jerked awake when he heard a baby cry.

But when he opened his eyes, there was no baby. Only his wife. Eyes still closed. Breath so faint that he had to stare hard at the pale blue–dotted gown covering her chest to be certain that it was moving.

"How is she?"

How many times had he heard the question? A dozen? Two? He focused on the petite woman standing inside the curtain. "Vivian? What're you doing here?"

"Checking on my granddaughter, of course." She slipped past him to peer closely at Greer. "You're a Templeton," she told her. "We're many things, but we're not weak." She kissed Greer's forehead, much like Meredith had, and straightened.

Her face seemed more lined. Wearier. He offered her the chair.

She took it and held her pocketbook on her lap with both hands. "I've spent so many days in my life at a hospital." She shook her head slightly and reached out to squeeze his hand. "It's Christmas Eve. Nothing's going to happen to our girl on Christmas Eve."

"That's what Carter said."

Her lips curved in a smile. Bittersweet. "He's like his father," she murmured.

Then it occurred to him. "Your party is tonight."

"It's on hold."

"Greer said you invited a hundred people."

She waved her fingers dismissively. "And they'll likely come when I reschedule. When you and Greer can both be there."

"I don't know if that's gonna happen," he admitted in a low voice.

She smiled gently. "I do." Then she pushed to her feet. "I've picked up Adelaide. She wanted me to see Greer first, but she's in the waiting room."

"That was nice of you, Vivian. Thank you."

"Don't get too sentimental on me. I have a selfish motivation, as well. She and Brutus will be coming home to stay with me. I convinced her to stay awhile." She reached up and patted his cheek. "And that's final, dear boy." Then she tugged on the hem of her nubby-looking pink suit and left.

Ryder moved back next to the bed. Greer's hand was cool when he picked it up. He pressed it to his mouth, warming it. He was still like that when he heard the curtain swish again.

Adelaide stood there.

He exhaled and lowered Greer's hand to the bed. Then he stood and let his aunt wrap her skinny, surprisingly strong arms around him. "You love her," she said in a whisper. He hadn't ever heard her speak so softly. "You need to tell her."

"How do you know I haven't?"

She pulled back and gave him a look out of those crazy made-up eyes of hers. "I've been living in the same house as the two of you for four months. How do you think I know?" Then she set a familiar-looking ring box in his hand.

He slid his jaw to one side. Then the other. "How'd you find it?"

Now she just looked droll. "You've always hidden your treasures in your sock drawer. Not very imaginative if I must say, and it was quite the nuisance getting past Layla's crib to get the drawer all the way open."

There was nothing to be amused about. Yet he still felt a faint smile lift his lips. Then he looked back at his wife. Lying in that bed.

And he closed his eyes.

"Ryder," Adelaide whispered. "Have faith."

"Faith hasn't gotten me very far before, Adelaide. You know that."

"You just weren't looking." She gestured toward the bed with her turquoise-laden hand. "What do you see when you look at her?"

My life.

"Tell her you love her. Give her your granny's ring. I know you said before that you were afraid to. Afraid she wouldn't want it. Wouldn't understand the treasure you were trying to give. This last thing that remains from your family." She squeezed his hand around the ring box. "And I'm telling you that she will." She went from squeezing his fingers to squeezing his jaw. "What do you *see* when you look at her, Ryder?"

His eyes burned. "My life."

She gave a great sigh and smiled. She pulled on his jaw until he lowered his head and she kissed his forehead, like she'd done about a million times before.

Then she, too, went back outside the curtain.

Ryder pushed open the ring box. The box alone was ancient. The filigreed diamond ring inside was from the

1920s. He slid it free from the fading blue velvet. It was so small it didn't fit over the tip of his finger.

He sat down beside the bed again. Slowly picked up Greer's hand. It was still cool. Too cool.

When they'd brought her to the hospital, they'd taken her jewelry. Her wedding band. Her earrings. Placed them in a plastic bag that they'd given to him. He wasn't sure where he'd even put it.

He slowly slid his grandmother's ring over Greer's wedding finger. He didn't expect it to fit. But it did. "With this ring," he whispered huskily.

"I thee wed." Her words were faint, her touch lighter than a whisper as she curled her fingers down over his.

His heart charged into his throat and he looked up at her face. Her eyes were barely open but a tear slid from the corner of her eye. "The baby..." Her lashes closed.

He leaned close and smoothed away that tear. "The baby's okay." His voice was rough. "You're okay. All you have to do is rest."

Her lashes lifted again. A little more this time. Her hand slowly rose. The back of her knuckles grazed his cheek. "You're crying. Just tell me the truth. The baby—"

"Is going to be okay."

Her eyes drifted closed again. "I should've told you." Another tear slid from her eye. "I'm so sorry I didn't tell you the truth."

"I should've seen." He cupped her head in his hand. "I should have seen all along. And you are the truth." He pressed his mouth against hers. "You're my truth. I just didn't let myself see it. You're my wife, Greer. For all the right reasons, you're my wife." He pulled in a shaky breath. "So just get better and come home with me and Layla. You can work any damn job you want. Just…don't give up on me. Don't give up on our family."

Her eyes opened again and she stared up at him. "I thought you gave up on me," she whispered.

"Not in this lifetime," he promised thickly. He pressed another shaking kiss to her lips, and her hand lifted, closing around his neck.

"Don't leave me."

He shook his head, but her eyes had closed again. He lowered the rail on the side of the bed. Carefully, gingerly, with the same caution he'd felt when he'd first taken Layla all those months ago, he moved her an inch. Two. Just enough that he could slide onto the edge of the hospital bed with her. It was crowded. He had to curl one arm awkwardly above her just to be sure that he wouldn't jostle her. Jostle their baby. But he managed.

"I love you, Greer."

She exhaled. Turned her head toward him. "Love… you…" Her fingers brushed his cheek. "No more great…divide."

A soft sound escaped him. "No more great divide," he promised. "Never again."

And then he closed his eyes, cradling his life against him.

And they both slept.

Epilogue

"Welcome home, Mrs. Wilson."

Greer smiled up at Ryder as he carried her across the threshold of their house. It was an interesting experience. He carried her. She carried Layla. "We could've walked, you know. The doctors said the baby was okay. So long as I don't try running a marathon, we're all good."

"I know." He shouldered the door closed behind him. "But then I wouldn't have this opportunity to impress my ladies with my manliness as we made the trek through the deep, freezing snow."

Greer pressed her cheek against his chest and looked at their daughter. "Daddy's very silly today. Two snowflakes. That's what we trekked through."

Layla's green eyes were bright. "Dadda!"

Ryder's dimple appeared. "Daddy's very happy today," he corrected. He carried the two of them right through the house and deposited them carefully on the couch. He peeled off his coat and pitched it aside, then sat down beside them, his fingers twining through Greer's. "It's Christmas Day and I've got the very best presents. Because Mommy's home."

"Mama!"

Greer went still. "Did she just—"

"She did. Who's Mama, Short-Stuff?"

"Mama." Layla patted Greer's cheek and pressed a wet kiss on it. Then she patted Ryder's face, kissing his clean-shaven jaw. "Dadda."

She clambered off Greer's lap and ran over to the oddly decorated Christmas tree. She started tearing into the wrapped presents beneath it. "Sus-suhs," she chanted.

"She's gonna demolish them all," Ryder commented.

"Probably." Greer slid her fingers through his and pulled his hand over the baby nestled inside her. "I wouldn't be too concerned. Most of them are hers, anyway. Between you and me and Adelaide, we might have gone a little overboard with the gifts."

"It's our first Christmas together. Overboard is expected."

"Now you sound like Vivian."

He grinned. "She rescheduled that party of hers for tomorrow night, you know. Just like that." He snapped his fingers.

"The advantages of outrageous wealth."

"Mama." Layla toddled back to the couch, her fists filled with the shreds of Christmas wrapping paper. She dropped it on Greer's lap.

"For me?"

Bright-eyed, Layla returned to the tree and started back in on the presents.

"We could go over to your parents', you know. Everyone's there. Hoping to see you."

She shook her head and wrapped her arms around his neck. "Maybe later. Right now…right now, everything I never even knew I wanted is right here."

His eyes smiled into hers. "Merry Christmas, Layla's mommy."

She smiled back. He thought he'd gotten the best gift. But she knew better. They'd all gotten the best gift. And she was going to treasure it for now and for always.

"Merry Christmas, Layla's daddy."

* * * * *

Make sure you didn't miss the other two stories starring Templeton triplets Maddie and Ali!

Yuletide Baby Bargain
Show Me a Hero

Part of New York Times *bestselling author Allison Leigh's Return to the Double C miniseries.*

Available from Harlequin Special Edition.

SPECIAL EXCERPT FROM

Turn the page for a sneak peek at New York Times
*bestselling author RaeAnne Thayne's next
heartwarming Haven Point romance,*
Season of Wonder,
available October 2018 from HQN Books!

*Dani Capelli and her daughters are
facing their first Christmas in Haven Point.
But Ruben Morales—the son of Dani's new boss—is
determined to give them a season of wonder!*

CHAPTER ONE

"THIS IS TOTALLY LAME. Why do we have to stay here and wait for you? We can walk home in, like, ten minutes."

Daniela Capelli drew in a deep breath and prayed for patience, something she seemed to be doing with increasing frequency these days when it came to her thirteen-year-old daughter. "It's starting to snow and already almost dark."

Silver rolled her eyes, something *she* did with increasing frequency these days. "So what? A little snow won't kill us. I would hardly even call that snow. We had way bigger storms than this back in Boston. Remember that big blizzard a few years ago, when school was closed for, like, a week?"

"I remember," her younger daughter, Mia, said, looking up from her coloring book at Dani's desk at the Haven Point Veterinary Clinic. "I stayed home from preschool and I watched Anna and Elsa a thousand times, until you said your eardrums would explode if I played it one more time."

Dani could hear a bark from the front office that likely signaled the arrival of her next client and knew she didn't have time to stand here arguing with an obstinate teenager.

"Mia can't walk as fast as you can. You'll end up frustrated with her and you'll both be freezing before you make it home," she pointed out.

"So she can stay here and wait for you while I walk home. I just told Chelsea we could FaceTime about the new dress she bought and she can only do it for another hour before her dad comes to pick her up for his visitation."

"Why can't you FaceTime here? I only have two more patients to see. I'll be done in less than an hour, then we can all go home together. You can hang out in the waiting room with Mia, where the Wi-Fi signal is better."

Silver gave a huge put-upon sigh but picked up her backpack and stalked out of Dani's office toward the waiting room.

"Can I turn on the TV out there?" Mia asked as she gathered her papers and crayons. "I like the dog shows."

The veterinary clinic showed calming clips of animals on a big flat-screen TV set low to the ground for their clientele.

"After Silver's done with her phone call, okay?"

"She'll take *forever*," Mia predicted with a gloomy look. "She always does when she's talking to Chelsea."

Dani fought to hide a smile. "Thanks for your patience, sweetie, with her and with me. Finish your math worksheet while you're here, then when we get home, you can watch what you want."

Both the Haven Point elementary and middle schools were within walking distance of the clinic and it had become a habit for Silver to walk to the elementary school and then walk with Mia to the clinic to spend a few hours until they could all go home together.

Of late, Silver had started to complain that she didn't want to pick her sister up at the elementary school every day, that she would rather they both just took their respective school buses home, where Silver could watch her sister without having to hang out at the boring veterinary clinic.

This working professional/single mother gig was *hard*, she thought as she ushered Mia to the waiting room. Then again, in most ways it was much easier than the veterinary student/single mother gig had been.

When they entered the comfortable waiting room—with its bright colors, pet-friendly benches and big fish tank—Mia faltered for a moment, then sidestepped behind Dani's back.

She saw instantly what had caused her daughter's nervous reaction. Funny. Dani felt the same way. She wanted to hide behind somebody, too.

The receptionist had given her the files with the dogs' names that were coming in for a checkup but hadn't mentioned their human was Ruben Morales. Her gorgeous next-door neighbor.

Dani's palms instantly itched and her stomach felt as if she'd accidentally swallowed a flock of butterflies.

"Deputy Morales," she said, then paused, hating the slightly breathless note in her voice.

What *was* it about the man that always made her so freaking nervous?

He was big, yes, at least six feet tall, with wide shoulders, tough muscles and a firm, don't-mess-with-me jawline.

It wasn't just that. Even without his uniform, the man exuded authority and power, which instantly raised her hackles and left her uneasy, something she found both frustrating and annoying about herself.

No matter how far she had come, how hard she had worked to make a life for her and her girls, she still sometimes felt like the troublesome foster kid from Queens.

She had done her best to avoid him in the months they had been in Haven Point, but that was next to impossible when they lived so close to each other—and when she was the intern in his father's veterinary practice.

"Hey, Doc," he said, flashing her an easy smile she didn't trust for a moment. It never quite reached his dark, long-lashed eyes, at least where she was concerned.

While she might be uncomfortable around Ruben Morales, his dogs were another story.

He held the leashes of both of them, a big, muscular Belgian shepherd and an incongruously paired little Chi-poo, and she reached down to pet both of them. They sniffed her and wagged happily, the big dog's tail nearly knocking over his small friend.

That was the thing she loved most about dogs. They were uncomplicated and generous with their affection, for the most part. They never looked at people with that subtle hint of suspicion, as if trying to uncover all their secrets.

"I wasn't expecting you," she admitted.

"Oh? I made an appointment. The boys both need

checkups. Yukon needs his regular hip and eye check and Ollie is due for his shots."

She gave the dogs one more pat before she straightened and faced him, hoping his sharp cop eyes couldn't notice evidence of her accelerated pulse.

"Your father is still here every Monday and Friday afternoons. Maybe you should reschedule with him," she suggested. It was a faint hope, but a girl had to try.

"Why would I do that?"

"Maybe because he's your father and knows your dogs?"

"Dad is an excellent veterinarian. Agreed. But he's also semiretired and wants to be fully retired this time next year. As long as you plan to stick around in Haven Point, we will have to switch vets and start seeing you eventually. I figured we might as well start now."

He was checking her out. Not *her* her, but her skills as a veterinarian.

The implication was clear. She had been here three months, and it had become obvious during that time in their few interactions that Ruben Morales was extremely protective of his family. He had been polite enough when they had met previously, but always with a certain guardedness, as if he was afraid she planned to take the good name his hardworking father had built up over the years for the Haven Point Veterinary Clinic and drag it through the sludge at the bottom of Lake Haven.

Dani pushed away her instinctive prickly defensiveness, bred out of all those years in foster care when she felt as if she had no one else to count on—compounded by the difficult years after she married Tommy and had Silver, when she *really* had no one else in her corner.

She couldn't afford to offend Ruben. She didn't need

his protective wariness to turn into full-on suspicion. With a little digging, Ruben could uncover things about her and her past that would ruin everything for her and her girls here.

She forced a professional smile. "It doesn't matter. Let's go back to a room and take a look at these guys. Girls, I'll be done shortly. Silver, keep an eye on your sister."

Her oldest nodded without looking up from her phone and with an inward sigh, Dani led the way to the largest of the exam rooms.

She stood at the door as he entered the room with the two dogs, then joined him inside and closed it behind her.

The large room seemed to shrink unnaturally and she paused inside for a moment, flustered and wishing she could escape. Dani gave herself a mental shake. She could handle being in the same room with the one man in Haven Point who left her breathless and unsteady.

All she had to do was focus on the reason he was here in the first place. His dogs.

She knelt to their level. "Hey there, guys. Who wants to go first?"

The Malinois wagged his tail again while his smaller counterpoint sniffed around her shoes, probably picking up the scents of all the other dogs she had seen that day.

"Ollie, I guess you're the winner today."

He yipped, his big ears that stuck straight out from his face quivering with excitement.

He was the funniest-looking dog, quirky and unique, with wisps of fur in odd places, spindly legs and a narrow Chihuahua face. She found him unbearably cute.

With that face, she wouldn't ever be able to say no to him if he were hers.

"Can I give him a treat?" She always tried to ask permission first from her clients' humans.

"Only if you want him to be your best friend for life," Ruben said.

Despite her nerves, his deadpan voice sparked a smile, which widened when she gave the little dog one of the treats she always carried in the pocket of her lab coat. He slurped it up in one bite, then sat with a resigned sort of patience during the examination.

She was aware of Ruben watching her as she carefully examined the dog, but Dani did her best not to let his scrutiny fluster her.

She knew what she was doing, she reminded herself. She had worked so hard to be here, sacrificing all her time, energy and resources of the last decade to nothing else but her girls and her studies.

"Everything looks good," she said after checking out the dog and finding nothing unusual. "He seems like a healthy little guy. It says here he's about six or seven. So you haven't had him from birth?"

"No. Only about two years. He was a stray I picked up off the side of the road between here and Shelter Springs when I was on patrol one day. He was in a bad way, half-starved, fur matted. As small as he is, it's a wonder he wasn't picked off by a coyote or even one of the bigger hawks. He just needed a little TLC."

"You couldn't find his owner?"

"We ran ads and Dad checked with all his contacts at shelters and veterinary clinics from here to Boise with no luck. I had been fostering him while we looked, and to be honest, I kind of lost my heart to the little guy, and by then Yukon adored him so we decided to keep him."

She was such a sucker for animal lovers, especially those who rescued the vulnerable and lost ones.

And, no, she didn't need counseling to point out the parallels to her own life.

Regardless, she couldn't let herself be drawn to Ruben and risk doing something foolish. She had too much to lose here in Haven Point.

"What about Yukon here?" She knelt down to examine the bigger dog. In her experience, sometimes bigger dogs didn't like to be lifted and she wasn't sure if the beautiful Malinois fell into that category.

Ruben shrugged as he scooped Ollie onto his lap to keep the little Chi-poo from swooping in and stealing the treat she held out for the bigger dog. "You could say he was a rescue, too."

"Oh?"

"He was a K-9 officer down in Mountain Home. After his handler was killed in the line of duty, I guess he kind of went into a canine version of depression and wouldn't work with anyone else. I know that probably sounds crazy."

She scratched the dog's ears, touched by the bond that could build between handler and dog. "Not at all," she said briskly. "I've seen many dogs go into decline when their owners die. It's not uncommon."

"For a year or so, they tried to match him up with other officers, but things never quite gelled, for one reason or another, then his eyes started going. His previous handler who died was a good buddy of mine from the academy, and I couldn't let him go just anywhere."

"Retired police dogs don't always do well in civilian

life. They can be aggressive with other dogs and some-times people. Have you had any problems with that?"

"Not with Yukon. He's friendly. Aren't you, buddy? You're a good boy."

Dani could swear the dog grinned at his owner, his tongue lolling out.

Yukon was patient while she looked him over, es-pecially as she maintained a steady supply of treats.

When she finished, she gave the dog a pat and stood. "Can I take a look at Ollie's ears one more time?"

"Sure. Help yourself."

He held the dog out and she reached for Ollie. As she did, the dog wriggled a little, and Dani's hands ended up brushing Ruben's chest. She froze at the accidental contact, a shiver rippling down her spine. She pinned her reaction on the undeniable fact that it had been en-tirely too long since she had touched a man, even ac-cidentally.

She had to cut out this *fascination* or whatever it was immediately. Clean-cut, muscular cops were *not* her type, and the sooner she remembered that the better.

She focused on checking the ears of the little dog, gave him one more scratch and handed him back to Ruben. "That should do it. A clean bill of health. You obviously take good care of them."

He patted both dogs with an affectionate smile that did nothing to ease her nerves.

"My dad taught me well. I spent most of my youth helping out here at the clinic—cleaning cages, brushing coats, walking the occasional overnight boarder. What-ever grunt work he needed. He made all of us help."

"I can think of worse ways to earn a dime," she said. The chance to work with animals would have been a dream opportunity for her, back when she had few bright spots in her world.

"So can I. I always loved animals."

She had to wonder why he didn't follow in his father's footsteps and become a vet. If he had, she probably wouldn't be here right now, as Frank Morales probably would have handed down his thriving practice to his own progeny.

Not that it was any of her business. Ruben certainly could follow any career path he wanted—as long as that path took him far away from her.

"Give me a moment to grab those medications and I'll be right back."

"No rush."

Out in the hall, she closed the door behind her and drew in a deep breath.

Get a grip, she chided herself. *He's just a hot-looking dude. Heaven knows you've had more than enough experience with those to last a lifetime.*

She went to the well-stocked medication dispensary, found what she needed and returned to the exam room.

Outside the door, she paused for only a moment to gather her composure before pushing it open. "Here are the pills for Ollie's nerves and a refill for Yukon's eyedrops," she said briskly. "Let me know if you have any questions—though if you do, you can certainly ask your father."

"Thanks." As he took them from her, his hands brushed hers again and sent a little spark of awareness shivering through her.

She was probably imagining the way his gaze sharpened, as if he had felt something odd, too.

"I can show you out. We're shorthanded today since

the veterinary tech and the receptionist both needed to leave early."

"No problem. That's what I get for scheduling the last appointment of the day—though, again, I spent most of my youth here. I think we can find our way."

"It's fine. I'll show you out." She stood outside the door while he gathered the dogs' leashes, then led the way toward the front office.

After three months, Ruben still couldn't get a bead on Dr. Daniela Capelli.

His next-door neighbor still seemed a complete enigma to him. By all reports from his father, she was a dedicated, earnest new veterinarian with a knack for solving difficult medical mysteries and a willingness to work hard. She seemed like a warm and loving mother, at least from the few times he had seen her interactions with her two girls, the uniquely named teenager Silver—who had, paradoxically, purple hair—and the sweet-as-Christmas-toffee Mia, who was probably about six.

He also couldn't deny she was beautiful, with slender features, striking green eyes, dark, glossy hair and a dusky skin tone that proclaimed her Italian heritage—as if her name didn't do the trick first.

He actually liked the trace of New York accent that slipped into her speech at times. It fitted her somehow, in a way he couldn't explain. Despite that, he couldn't deny that the few times he had interacted with more than a wave in passing, she was brusque, prickly and sometimes downright distant.

His father adored her and wouldn't listen to a negative thing about her.

You just have to get to know her, Frank had said the other night. He apparently didn't see how diligently Dani Capelli worked to keep anyone else from doing just that.

She wasn't unfriendly, only distant. She kept herself to herself. Did Dani have any idea how fascinated the people of Haven Point were with these new arrivals in their midst?

Or maybe that was just him.

As he followed her down the hall in her white lab coat, his dogs behaving themselves for once, Ruben told himself to forget about his stupid attraction to her.

When they walked into the clinic waiting room, they found her two girls there. The older one was texting on her phone while her sister did somersaults around the room.

Dani stopped in the doorway and seemed to swallow an exasperated sound. "Mia, honey, you're going to have dog hair all over you."

"I'm a snowball rolling down the hill," the girl said. "Can't you see me getting bigger and bigger and bigger?"

He could tell the moment the little girl spotted him and his dogs coming into the area behind her mother. She went still and then slowly rose to her feet, features shifting from gleeful to nervous.

Why was she so afraid of him?

"You make a very good snowball," he said, pitching his voice low and calm as his father had taught him to do with all skittish creatures. "I haven't seen anybody somersault that well in a long time."

She moved to her mother's side and buried her face in Dani's white coat—though he didn't miss the way she reached down to pet Ollie on her way.

"Hey again, Silver."

He knew the older girl from the middle school, where he served as the resource officer a few hours a week. He made it a point to learn all the students' names and tried to talk to them individually when he had the chance, in hopes that if they had a problem they would feel comfortable coming to him.

He had the impression that Silver was like her mother in many ways. Reserved, wary, slow to trust. It made him wonder just who had hurt them.

Don't miss Season of Wonder
by RaeAnne Thayne,
available October 2018
wherever HQN books and ebooks are sold!

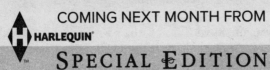

Get 4 FREE REWARDS!

We'll send you 2 FREE Books plus <u>2</u> FREE Mystery Gifts.

Harlequin® Special Edition books feature heroines finding the balance between their work life and personal life on the way to finding true love.

FREE Value Over $20

YES! Please send me 2 FREE Harlequin® Special Edition novels and my 2 FREE gifts (gifts are worth about $10 retail). After receiving them, if I don't wish to receive any more books, I can return the shipping statement marked "cancel." If I don't cancel, I will receive 6 brand-new novels every month and be billed just $4.99 per book in the U.S. or $5.74 per book in Canada. That's a savings of at least 12% off the cover price! It's quite a bargain! Shipping and handling is just 50¢ per book in the U.S. and 75¢ per book in Canada*. I understand that accepting the 2 free books and gifts places me under no obligation to buy anything. I can always return a shipment and cancel at any time. The free books and gifts are mine to keep no matter what I decide.

235/335 HDN GMY2

Name (please print)

Address   Apt. #

City   State/Province   Zip/Postal Code

Mail to the **Reader Service:**
IN U.S.A.: P.O. Box 1341, Buffalo, NY 14240-8531
IN CANADA: P.O. Box 603, Fort Erie, Ontario L2A 5X3

Want to try two free books from another series? Call 1-800-873-8635 or visit www.ReaderService.com.

SPECIAL EXCERPT FROM

H HARLEQUIN®

SPECIAL EDITION

*Tamara Owens is supposed to be finding the person
stealing from her father. But when she meets prime
suspect Flint Collins—and his new charge, Diamond—
she can't bear to pull away, despite her tragic past.
Will Flint be able to look past her lies to make them a
family by Christmas?*

*Read on for a sneak preview of
the next book in The Daycare Chronicles,*
An Unexpected Christmas Baby
by USA TODAY *bestselling author Tara Taylor Quinn.*

How hadn't he heard her first knock?

And then she saw the carrier on the chair next to him. He'd
been rocking it.

"What on earth are you doing to that baby?" she exclaimed,
nothing in mind but to rescue the child in obvious distress.

"Damned if I know," he said loudly enough to be heard
over the noise. "I fed her, burped her, changed her. I've done
everything they said to do, but she won't stop crying."

Tamara was already unbuckling the strap that held the
crying infant in her seat. She was so tiny! Couldn't have been
more than a few days old. There were no tears on her cheeks.

"There's nothing poking her. I checked," Collins said,
not interfering as she lifted the baby from the seat, careful to
support the little head.

It wasn't until that warm weight settled against her that
Tamara realized what she'd done. She was holding a baby.
Something she couldn't do.

She was going to pay. With a hellacious nightmare at the
very least.

The baby's cries had stopped as soon as Tamara picked her up.

"What did you do?" Collins was there, practically touching her, he was standing so close.

"Nothing. I picked her up."

"There must've been some problem with the seat, after all..." He'd tossed the infant head support on the desk and was removing the washable cover.

"I'm guessing she just wanted to be held," Tamara said. What the hell was she doing?

Tearless crying generally meant anger, not physical distress. And why did Flint Collins have a baby in his office?

She had to put the child down. But couldn't until he put the seat back together. The newborn's eyes were closed and she hiccuped and then sighed.

Clenching her lips for a second, Tamara looked away. "Babies need to be held almost as much as they need to be fed," she told him while she tried to understand what was going on.

He was checking the foam beneath the seat cover and the straps, too. He was fairly distraught himself.

Not what she would've predicted from a hard-core businessman possibly stealing from her father.

"Who is she?" she asked, figuring it was best to start at the bottom and work her way up to exposing him for the thief he probably was.

He straightened. Stared at the baby in her arms, his brown eyes softening and yet giving away a hint of what looked like fear at the same time. In that second she wished like hell that her father was wrong and Collins wouldn't turn out to be the one who was stealing from Owens Investments.

Don't miss
An Unexpected Christmas Baby *by Tara Taylor Quinn,*
available November 2018 wherever
Harlequin® Special Edition books and ebooks are sold.

www.Harlequin.com

Looking for more satisfying love stories
with community and family at their core?

Check out **Harlequin® Special Edition**
and **Love Inspired®** books!

 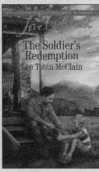

New books available every month!

CONNECT WITH US AT:

Facebook.com/groups/HarlequinConnection

 Facebook.com/HarlequinBooks

 Twitter.com/HarlequinBooks

 Instagram.com/HarlequinBooks

 Pinterest.com/HarlequinBooks

ReaderService.com

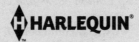

**ROMANCE WHEN
YOU NEED IT**

HFGENRE2018